DEATH
BY
ASSOCIATION

ERNEST
MORRIS

GOOD 2 GO PUBLISHING

DEATH BY ASSOCIATION
Written by Ernest Morris
Cover Design: Davida Baldwin, Odd Ball Designs
Typesetter: Mychea
ISBN: 9781947340572
Copyright © 2020 Good2Go Publishing
Published 2020 by Good2Go Publishing
7311 W. Glass Lane • Laveen, AZ 85339
www.good2gopublishing.com
https://twitter.com/good2gobooks
G2G@good2gopublishing.com
www.facebook.com/good2gopublishing
www.instagram.com/good2gopublishing

PROLOGUE

LO'S EYES GOT WATERY AS HE WAS CHARGED BY HIS eight-year-old son, Money. It'd' been two years since he had held his entire family in his arms. Caught in a trance as his eyes locked on his beautiful wife, Lo nearly lost his balance as Money hugged him like he was a football player, defending his turf like his daddy taught him.

"Daddy, I missed you," yelled Money.

Lo could see the excitement in each of their eyes, but deep down in his mind he knew that his family was trying their hardest not to crack and show any emotion as they held it together.

"I missed you too," Lo said to Money as he gave him a tight hug and a kiss on top of his head. It was a habit he had inherited from his brother.

The rest of his family waited patiently to be greeted. As Lo released his bear hug grip from his dad, Lo went down the line greeting his beautiful family.

"King, what's up, boy?" Lo said as he hugged and kissed his oldest son on the forehead. He was just as excited to see his father as his father was. By the time Lo released his hug with King, he was embraced by his twin daughters, Belle and Bella. They couldn't wait any longer to finally touch their fathers' skin.

"Hey, Daddy," they both shouted simultaneously.

"What happened to my baby girls?" Lo said as his daughters clutched him on each side.

In two years, Lo couldn't believe how much his daughters had grown up. As they released their embrace, Lo grabbed his beautiful wife, his queen, the mother of his child, and began to kiss her. It felt like forever since he felt the love from his wife Lyla. His body melted in her arms, just like the first time they had sex on her mother's sofa.

After they were seated, his kids ran down the past two years that he missed of their lives. Belle and Bella rambled on and on about cheerleading practice, while King and Money shared their football stories.

As they spoke about their second Thanksgiving without their father and how there was an empty seat at the dinner table, that was the first reminder of his broken family. Lo's kids held strong not to let a tear fall, but Money couldn't hold back his tears as they ripped through his cornea.

"It's going to be alright," Lo said, wiping away Money's tears. "Daddy will be home soon."

They all smiled with joy, but deep down inside Lo knew that he was lying. That was the one thing he hated doing, lying to his family. He looked at Lyla, and her face said it all. He knew that she hadn't broken the news to the kids.

ONE

IT WAS A CONSTANT BATTLE IN THE HOLE, A CONSTANT back-and-forth. Cars pulled up with three or four guys running to the vehicle trying to get to the front seat. Then half a block down the street, they were jumping out screaming for the next vic. From a neighbor's perspective, it looked like a track meet. To most, it was the *chase*, the chase to catch a vic, also known as a *fiend*. Some called them *vics* (short for victims, fiends, crackheads, and smokers), but Lo called them *DFs* (dope fiends). He always wanted to be different from everybody else.

All day long in the Hole, you would see young and older men chasing cars. Some old and rusty, ready to fall apart, and some nice, new and clean. You could almost tell what kind of money a DF would spend by the type of car they drove, but looks could be deceiving. You had to watch out for vice. Any new car or unknown DFs would always be interrogated before a sale was made.

Questions like, "Where you from?" "Who you know?" "Are you a cop?" Then, "Where's your pipe?" They would have new DFs smoke in front of them before they were labeled official.

The Hole wasn't like other drug areas in Allentown. You couldn't just post up or set up shop and make sales in the Hole. You had to be born and raised up there. So when you were ready to hustle, the doors were always open. Not too many outsiders entered the Hole either, let alone hustled. There were two well-known suppliers, born and raised, who supplied the hustlers. They were cousins Diesel and Rock. Only in their twenties, some considered them as their old heads, but Lo considered them as his guide and steppingstone.

Lo was young, but very mature for his age. He hung around all the older people, soaking in their knowledge of the streets and drug game. He watched how they moved and interacted with the customers. Most of them were behind the project row homes when they served a fiend.

Hand to hand was a common thing to Lo. It took him back to age ten when he first witnessed his father doing the same thing in the bottom of the Hole, known as the Oil. The old heads were more cautious because the park sat dead center of the Hole, and from a distance in any direction you could spot a drug sale.

The park consisted of two full basketball courts centered in the middle of several homes on each of its four sides. It literally sat on its own island. As drug-infested as it was, the park was its main attraction. Everything went down there: basketball, football, baseball, cookouts, smoking, drinking, and its main course, drug dealing.

The old heads considered Lo and his crew as young boys. They would send them on runs to the store to buy

Dutches and drinks. If they had any beef with anyone younger than them, the young boys would attack, no questions asked. They were also lookouts for the police. It was everybody's duty to notify each other if police were in the vicinity, so they could hide the drugs and money if they had to.

They would use empty juice cartons, chip bags or any other garbage that sat on the ground. The old heads had a lot of love for the young boys because they knew that eventually they would take their place in the drug game, and the generation after them would be doing the same.

At the young age of thirteen, Lo was plotting his way in the game. Not only did he take notes from the old heads, but he also watched his older brother Mack and analyzed his moves. Lo waited for his moment. He knew he had to crawl before he walked and walk before he ran, and when he ran, his run would be like no other.

At fourteen Mack got real familiar with the law. He was

arrested and charged with strong-arm robbery and sat in Dorneyville's Detention Center for Juveniles for two weeks. He was then released and placed on house arrest. Before the run-in with the law, he had a partner in crime named Ricky. Ricky was big and cocky to be fourteen.

He was five foot six, 130 pounds, and rock solid. Early in their youth they were known as the Diablo brothers on the football field. Coaches hated going against their defense at LCYA. They were compared to the '85 Bears. On offense, Mack played tailback and Ricky played fullback. On defense they played side by side, middle linebacker. They were two of the most vicious players to ever play in the area. At thirteen they both were offered full scholarships to play football for the best high school team in the city, Central Catholic.

With no guidance or family support, as most under-privileged kids, they turned it down. They had their eyes set on another love, another sport—a sport that sucks the soul out of a man. It was the sport of hustling. Mack and

Ricky witnessed the money, cars, jewelry, women and other things, and wanted parts of that life, the street life. The life that sometimes always seems right to a man, but the end of it leads to DEATH.

Big T had seen the hunger in the two young boys' eyes, and he put them on. Big T was one of the originals from the Hole. He was a branch off of Diesel and Rock's family tree. He supplied Mack and Ricky with packs of dope and demanded a 75/25 split.

While Mack and Ricky was making crazy money for Big T, they caught the attention of a more powerful hustler, one of the cofounders of the Hole. People in the streets feared him. His name was Zeus, and he was a black Cuban Moro who looked like he had done a bid in a state penitentiary somewhere. Zeus was six foot two with arms like Hulk Hogan. He resembled Debo from one of those *Friday* movies.

Zeus witnessed a beating Mack and Ricky put on a

smoker who tried to rob him. They heard him tell the smoker that when he caught him, he was dead, and knew that he had been robbed. As soon as the smoker got within arm's reach, Ricky sent a straight jab stopping the smoker in his tracks. His head snapped back like he hit a brick wall. Mack followed with a two-piece, knocking him unconscious.

The two of them continued stomping and punching him until Zeus arrived. Ever since that day, Zeus spoke highly of the duo and tried to put them on his team. He talked to them multiple times about joining his team and supplying the young thugs. Mack liked the part about supplying them, but joining his team was a whole different story. In his mind, that was not happening.

Zeus's team consisted of three people. His right-hand man, Willie; his nephew Big Poppa; and Big Poppa's right-hand man, Pretty Boy. Zeus was the muscle, while Willie was the brains. Big Poppa and Pretty Boy ran a part of Center City. Zeus knew his team was thorough, but fifty

7

goons wasn't as thorough as the two young stallions. They were bosses on the rise, and he wanted no part of them unless they were on his team.

Even though they worked for Big T, he wanted them on his full payroll. He tried to entice them with his big truck with the sound system, rims, and jewelry, and flossed some cash in their face trying to persuade them. It didn't work.

Growing up with everything, then having it stripped from you, you try to accumulate all your loses in a matter of days. The ambition was in Mack's eyes. All the material shit, he cared less about. He was chasing the money. Rumor was that he spent up to fifteen hours a day on the block. He would skip school just to be out there grinding. Mack ended up taking Zeus's offer and was being sup-lied by both Zeus and Big T. You would catch Mack and Ricky riding in Zeus's Yukon Denali all around the Hole.

No one knew their deal. They all assumed that the

duo was putting in work for him and stayed out their way. In the hood most old heads would pay the young boys to do their dirty work. Since Mack and Ricky feared no one, the picture fit the lens. To them, putting in work was like riding a bike: once you learn how to handle the machine, the rest is cake. Mack was five foot five and rock solid. He packed a punch like Mike Tyson, thanks to his cousin Rob.

Rob was married to Mack's cousin Jessica. They moved to the Oil from New York in the early '90s. Every weekend while growing up Rob taught his little cousins how to box. But in the mid-'90s, the guns got involved, so the pull of the trigger became more popular. Mack and Ricky had two twin Desert Eagles. Whether they could handle the kickback from the powerful weapons was still unknown, but the size of the guns alone scared a bear.

At fifteen, Mack wasn't a pushover. He knew what Zeus's intentions were, but Zeus didn't know his. Zeus saw Mack as a soldier, a flunky, and Mack saw him as an asset. Mack had a vision: he saw a bigger picture, and in his mind, he drew up a master plan. His plan was to get rich, or die trying, all for the love of the mighty dollar.

TWO

BOOM!

The sound of Mack kicking the door off its hinges echoed through the house. Johnny jumped out of his seat as he saw the masked man enter with his gun drawn. The size of the gun nearly made him piss his pants. Zeus put Mack and Ricky onto a jux. The target was a kingpin named Rico and his worker. Rico was well respected in the city, and nobody dared to fuck with him. Rico owned a bodega on Fifth Street, a rim mechanic shop under the Hamilton Street Bridge and a barbershop on Ninth Street. He supplied 95 percent of the city with cocaine, dope, marijuana.

"Get the fuck on the floor," Mack yelled, waving his Desert Eagle.

Johnny got on his knees with his hands up. From the reflection off Mack's chrome cannon, Ricky noticed

Johnny complying with Mack and noticed none of the neighbors gave mind to the loud bang. Ricky emerged into the house with his gun drawn. Once Johnny saw two masked men with their guns, he lowered his head in defeat. He knew he had gotten caught slipping. Mack noticed the scattered money on the kitchen table wrapped in rubber bands, but what they had come for, the brick of coke, wasn't in sight.

"Where the fuck the work at?" Ricky demanded.

"Wha . . . wha . . . coke?" Johnny stuttered.

"Playing dumb is only gonna get you hurt," Ricky stated, getting agitated as he invaded Johnny's personal space. Ricky was so close to Johnny's face, he could smell Ricky's foul odor.

"I'm only gonna ask you one more time. Where. Is. The. Fucking. Work?"

Before Johnny had the chance to say something slick out his mouth, Mack slid the butt of his gun across his cranium. Blood trickled down his face. "Where is it at?"

Johnny lay flat on his chest stretched out like he was dead. Without lifting his head, he pointed toward the closet. Mack headed in that direction, cautiously just in case it was a trap.

"It better not be a trap, or you're dead," Ricky said with venom in his voice.

Mack yanked open the closet door. It was empty. On the floor sat a green book bag. He unzipped the bag and saw what they had come there for. The brick was neatly wrapped.

"Bingo," Mack said as he turned around grinning inside his ski mask. He walked toward the dining room table and deposited the scattered money into the bag.

Mack laughed as he told Lo the story. Puppet was asleep when he heard a stampede of footsteps running up the stairs. As he walked into the hallway, he caught Mack and Ricky entering the room with a book bag in hand. By the time Lo reached Mack's room, they had money scattered on his bed.

"How much money is there?" Lo asked as Mack finished his story.

Mack glanced at his lil brother's eyes and said, "I'm not sure yet, but it's not enough." Lo's eyes glowed as he stared at the money. Scrooge McDuck was floating through his mind. "Look, lil bro, I do all the hard work, so one day none of us will have to work. We gonna start our own family business. You just focus on school because this money here is going for your college degree."

Lo was a straight-A student before his father went to jail. His grades started to decline in every subject except for math. Mack knew that Lo's gift from God was in those numbers. Mack's plan was to put his lil brother through college so he would be the one to run the family business. He was going to major in business management. Lo enjoyed his big brother's speech and smiled at his college comments, but the only thing on his mind was the money.

"Man, let's count this money," Ricky chimed in, anxious to get his cut. "Y'all doing all that talking about college and shit; use that brain and start counting."

After unwrapping all the rubber bands, separating the fives, tens, twenties, fifties, and hundreds, there were twenty-five thousand dollars sitting on the bed.

"Look, Ricky, with all money, we can split it half and half, twelve, five a piece. Or we can buy our own brick and start our own movement. No more fronts from Big T or Zeus. What you think about that, partner?"

From the look on Ricky's face, Mack could tell he wasn't seeing the bigger picture. He looked confused. He couldn't comprehend Mack's plan or his vision to run their own organization.

"Just give me my half and I'll let you know in a couple of days," said Ricky.

Mack knew exactly what Ricky would say. He knew that he wouldn't be able to handle all that money. Mack was always two steps ahead of the game. He saved up every dollar from the packs he pushed, wishing on a break. He was good without Ricky's half. Mack pushed his half to the side of the bed.

"Here's twelve five. Don't spend it all in one place."

Ricky laughed as he stuffed the money in his pants pockets. He gave Mack some dap and saluted Lo from afar as he exited the room with a smile on his face. Mack shook his head in disappointment. He looked at Lo then continued their conversation.

"Bro, niggas like that fall off quick or get jammed up for flashing. You'll see."

Lo listened while keeping his eye on the money. He thought about how easy it was to come up. "Mack, put me on, bro," he said without realizing what he said. Mack looked up and gave him a death stare.

"Do you know the consequences of this game? It's nothing like you ever experienced," Mack stated.

"Ahhhhh, yeah, I know what it means. Get money, buy cars, dress nice, jewelry, and whatever else I want. Oh, and I can't forget about fucking bitches."

"Not quite, lil bro. You're missing two key points about this lifestyle: DEATH and JAIL. If you think this shit is all fun and games, you have another fucking thing coming. This shit will give all the things you said, but it can also end all of that in the blink of an eye. You'll go to jail or die in these streets all alone."

"Okay! You can at least think about it," Lo said. Mack just ignored him and made some phone calls.

Lo was up all night. He couldn't sleep because all he could think about was the money, he'd seen his brother with. He envisioned Jordans, Air Forces, Polo shirts, and Levi jeans. He thought to himself how he would be the flyest thirteen-year-old in middle school. All the girls would be on his dick if they knew he had money in his pockets. He thought about his mother working two jobs just to support him and his siblings. He hated to ask her for money. He thought about how he could make money, and the only thing that came to his mind was hustling.

~ ~ ~

School was out, and Lo closed his locker and headed to the flagpole to meet his squad, the young boys. Waiting there was Nico, his lil brother AR, Frisk, Juan Pepe, his cousin Fee, Mello, Logan and his best friend Primo. Mello, Logan, and Primo were the youngest of the young boys. Logan was the little brother of Big T; Mello's dad was Zeus; and Primo was the lil cousin to Diesel and Rock. They were born certified.

As Lo walked to the flagpole, he saw Logan and giggled as he thought about the night before when he and his squad snuck into Hickory Manor's basketball game. The young boys got caught and were immediately kicked out. But before they exited the school, Logan ran back to the gym, locked the doors, and shouted through the crack something obscene. They all busted out laughing in tears and clowned Logan the entire walk to the Hole. Logan didn't give a shit. He shrugged his shoulders and picked his wedgie from his sweatpants and laughed.

Nobody fucked with the Hole's young boys. Their old heads put in so much work throughout their childhood, the streets feared them, and they ran Hickory Manor. Lo dapped them up as he was the last to arrive.

"What's up with you niggas?"

"Ain't shit. We chilling waiting on you."

They made sure their whole squad was there before strolling to the Hole. During their walks they would target victims, especially someone riding a bike. They would jump them if they didn't give it up. Even the high school kids got a taste of the young thugs. Everyone but Lo lived in the Hole. While they all went home to report to their parents, he would sit in the park and watch the old heads hustle. He always felt like he was ahead of the game, as much time as he spent analyzing. He took heed to everything the older generation said.

"Go hard or go home, youngin. Stack that bread, young boy," one dude used to tell him.

At thirteen, he didn't fully understand what they meant, but soon he'd figure out. At six o'clock, the Hole's Boys and Girls Club was the place to be. That's where you would find Lo and the young boys at. They played basketball, football, ping-pong, billiards, and bumper pool. The center was run by Kevin. As much time as Kevin spent with the kids, he practically raised them all. He watched them grow from green cards, to blue, yellow, and then orange. There were three other Boys and Girls Clubs in the city. Sixth Street, Lil Creek, and the Hole's biggest rivals, the Garden Gorilla's Boys and Girls Club. Even though Lo's family lived up there, when it came to sports, his loyalty was to the Hole.

Along with the fellas were the project females. Lo's longtime on-and-off girlfriend was Jazzy. She was Promo's older sister. She was so beautiful that all the boys around the projects used to sweat her. Just a few inches shorter than Lo, she had caramel skin, light brown eyes and a nice round butt. People knew that Lo was in love, but he never showed it. Jazzy had two cousins, Kim and Sandy, who were sisters. Kim was dating Juan Pepe. She was his biggest fan and supporter. Sandy had a crush on Lo. Every time Jazzy was away, she would try to push up on him.

Then there was Jenny and Jessica; Mary, who was best friends with Lo's cousin Kate; and Te Te, who was best friends with Jazz's other cousin Lisa. Lisa was Rock's little sister. Then there was Heather. Until eight thirty this was the young boys' hangout spot where they enjoyed their youth, until Lo changed the game . . .

THREE

THREE DAYS WENT BY, AND MACK STILL HADN'T
heard from Ricky. He'd been calling and paging, even
using his emergency code, 187, which meant homicide.
After twenty minutes of waiting, his phone went off.

"Damn, nigga, where the fuck you been? I've been
blowing you up for a minute."

Ricky sensed Mack's anger. "Chill, bro. I've been here
at Big Poppa's spot with his peoples trying to snatch up a
few heavy hitters."

Mack's reply was simple and straight to the point.
"Have you thought about what we talked about yet?"

"Yeah, but I kind of dipped into it. Mom was backed
up on bills and shit, and I had to help her out. Then I
treated myself to a few things."

"A few things," Mack thought. "I feel you. Gotta take

care of home first. Holla at me later then," Mack said, then hung up.

He knew that only half of Ricky's story was true. And the part about him helping his mom, Mack knew he was full of shit. He didn't let that distract him. He had a vision, and Ricky couldn't see it. He had always involved Ricky in all his moves. Like the time they ran up on this young boy on Seventeenth and Gordon. The kid was flossing the new iPhone, and they caught him slipping. They ended up selling the phone for $200 dollars and splitting the profit down the middle. This plan was no different.

Mack knew that Zeus was easily influencing Ricky. Ricky didn't catch on to Zeus's manipulation, flashing the glitz and glamour, but Mack caught on instantly. Compared to Big T, Zeus was killing the streets. He had the big truck and jewelry and flashed his money around town, while Big T was a family man that drove a Nissan Armada SUV. Little by little Ricky was shitting on the person who put him on to chase his own dream. Mack was built and ready for those types of naysayers. So he played his position and stood firm to the slogan that he knew: "Never bite the hand that feeds you."

No one knew about the extra tip that Mack and Ricky received from the jux. Slowly word got out that Zeus was the prime suspect. A brick and twenty-five grand was taken from the boss. Rico was humble about his illegal business, but his presence spoke money. His wardrobe always consisted of the finest three-piece suits and loafers, resembling James Bond. Once Mack caught wind of the latest gossip, he took a step back from Zeus. There are rules to the game, and one of them is you can't get money and beef at the same damn time. So Mack remained low-key, plotting on his power move. One day while paying Big T for his usual zip, Mack decided to pick his brain.

"Yo, T, how much for a half, man?" he asked, catching him off guard.

Big T looked at Mack as if he was speaking a foreign language. "What you need all that weight for? You know that's a grip. You'll have to move a lot more dubs and save your entire profit," Big T said, trying to belittle him.

He knew every dollar Mack could make off each zip that was given to him and knew that it would take another six months to reach that amount. But what Big T didn't know was that Mack was pushing work for him and Zeus, and thanks to the jux, Mack's chips were up.

"I just want to set a goal so I can be in a better position. I ain't trying to push zips for the rest of my life."

"I feel you, youngin. Come back to me when you're closer to the twenty mark; then we can talk some business."

"Twenty for a half a man?" Mack thought. "Say no more." In the back of his mind he knew Big T was trying to profit heavy off him. He was just another crab in the bucket. Once a crab tries to get out, another crab is right there to bring him down. Big T was trying to keep Mack as a worker, but he wasn't having it. He was a boss. He chuckled at Big T's remarks. He was a little disappointed, but he continued to stay two steps ahead of the game. He just had to cut the middleman out, and he knew just who to talk to.

Mack texted Zeus as he stopped at Erica's house. She was his girlfriend, and a money-hungry project chick from the Oil. Mack knew, but he just used her for sex and to stash his work at her crib. As soon as he greeted Erica with a kiss, his cellphone rang.

"Zeus, what's good?"

"What's cracking, young boy?" Zeus was speaking in his Cuban accent.

"I need to holla at you ASAP. Business. I'm at my shorty's crib."

"Be there in ten minutes."

Erica was eavesdropping on their whole conversation

and freaked out when he ended his call. "You only been here for two fucking minutes and you're already leaving? Who you fucking, Mack? I haven't seen you in a week. Where the fuck have you been?"

"I'm not fucking anyone but you," Mack replied, being caught off guard. "Furthermore, lower your voice, ma, when you're talking to me. I've been out here trapping. I told you that I gotta make this money. Here's two hundred dollars. Go do something and I'll be back." Mack knew that would be the only way to shut her up. She placed the money in her bra. She hugged him and began to kiss him. As they kissed, Erica grabbed his dick and started massaging it. The sound of the car horn ended what was about to happen. "I'll be back, ma, I promise."

Mack placed his work inside Erica's dresser and put his gun on his waist. She watched him leave her house and hop into Zeus's truck. Mack stretched out his fist and gave Zeus the Hole's signature greeting.

"What's good with you? Is everything alright?"

"Everything is good. Let's get out of here," Mack said, leaning back in his seat a little. As Zeus pulled off, Mack's phone buzzed indicating that he had a text message. A familiar number came across the screen. He read the text, then continued talking to Zeus. "Look, I've been trying to make a move, and I wanted to know if you would be able to service me?"

"What do you need? Speak up, a closed mouth don't get fed," Zeus said, giving him his full attention.

"I'm trying to cop some weight."

"Oh, okay! What are you looking to buy, an ounce or two?"

Mack felt like Zeus was trying to play him like he was a flunky. "An ounce or two," Mack laughed. "Na, but if you're speaking in those terms, how about eighteen ounces? A half a man."

Zeus's eyes lit up. "Half a man?" Before Mack could

respond, Zeus went into the same spiel Big T had. "You don't have to spend your money, lil nigga. That's why I'm here. All you gotta do is keep stacking your bread and I got you."

Mack refused to talk back. He let Zeus continue to try to run game, while he sat in his seat looking out the window. Zeus then spoke about Rico and another lick he had lined up. Mack entertained his conversation like he was interested. He wasn't focused on being his muscle, let alone being on his team. Zeus knew he had Ricky locked in, and he tried to lock in Mack. Ricky had heart, but he didn't have the brains like Mack. Mack saw right through Zeus. He needed thorough flunkies.

Zeus was trying to treat Mack like a side ho that he took to McDonald's. Then he dropped him off at the crib. When they got home, Mack exited the SUV, and Zeus expressed himself one last time.

"Let me know about that lick."

"No doubt. I got you," Mack said as he shut the door.

Mack shook his head as he walked off. He knew Zeus only wanted what was best for himself. Mack knew he had to distance himself from him and if Ricky wanted to fuck with him, then that was on him. As of now, it was fuck Zeus.

FOUR

IT WAS FRIDAY, AND SCHOOL WAS FINALLY OUT.

Lo had heard that his homie Frisk got into a rumble at the gym. Word was that he fought a nigga from Second. So he knew they probably would be waiting for him outside after school. Frisk was a wild son of a bitch on the fight game. He would always pick fights with Terry, knowing that he wouldn't fight him because he would have to fight Frisk's older brother Muzzle.

Lo, always being on point, notified his team to switch up their meeting point to Chestnut instead of the flagpole. Chestnut was a side alley next to the H.M. Once they arrived, they noticed a few cats from Second huddled up. Lo and the young boys weren't exactly sure who Frisk had fought, but word was it was a kid named MC.

Lo only knew of one MC, Ronald Rowland. He would catch Ronald rapping in the hallway and would yell out that the emcee was coming. It sort of stuck with him after that. MC had an older brother named Mark. He was well respected on Second Street. They called him Mark because he would mark his targets. They would either get jumped, shot, or stabbed.

Lo caught the eyes of MC staring at his crew as they walked through their territory. From afar, Lo noticed one of MC's eyes were swollen, which must have come from the fight.

"Yo, there them niggas from the Hole," MC yelled. Lo knew that some shit was about to pop off, but Logan was the first to respond.

"Yeah, what's cracking?" MC started walking toward them with his homies trailing.

"Tell that nigga Frisk when we get off this suspension, it's on. That pussy wanna sneak me when we was leaving the gym. That's some sucka shit."

"Why don't you tell him yourself?" Logan responded,

then threw the first punch and caught MC square on his jaw and he buckled. AR grabbed MC's boy by his shirt as he tried to run from the fight, and slammed him up against the wall.

Lo scooped MC up off his feet and slammed him to the ground, then wailed punches on his face. It was a royal rumble on Chestnut. There were two niggas from the Hole on each one of the Second Street niggas. Lo and the young boys noticed that they were laid out, so they ran from the scene.

The young boys laughed and joked about how they had the Second Street dudes crying and screaming for help as they skated up to the woods and stopped at George's. George's was a small bodega that sat at the edge of the woods, inside of the Hole. He sold everything from cell phones, papers, hoagies, and cheesesteaks, to burgers and fries. Occasionally he would sell pastelillos and Spanish food. On nice days you could find all the young boys posted up on milk crates, chilling outside of the bodega.

Old heads called that spot "Cutthroat Island." While
Lo and his boys sat on crates munching on french fries,
he noticed two fiends walking out of the woods, heading
toward the park. They were regular customers who
bought crack every day.

"Damn," Lo yelled out.

"What happened?" Cee asked, jumping off the crate
scared.

"If I had some work, I could have made them sales."
Everyone looked at Lo in shock.

"Are you serious?" asked AR. He was staring at him
like he was crazy.

"Yeah! I'm trying to get this money. All you gotta do is
sit here and wait. They'll come to you."

"Nigga, you're only thirteen. Nobody's gonna buy
drugs off of you. If anything, they'll try to steal your shit,"

AR said, causing the others to laugh.

AR had a point, but Lo brushed it off. In his mind he knew he was ready, and he wanted to have the Hole on lock. Lo kept quiet and went into his thoughts. He continued to eat his french fries as his team scattered one by one. The last to leave was his closest friend J.P.

"Are you going to the gym at six thirty?" Lo asked. He said yeah. "Alright, I'll see you there." Lo stepped off and headed toward the park to see if he spotted Mack.

It was Friday, so he figured he would be posted up on the corner somewhere. Once he got to the yellow poles, he noticed that they were running a full-court game of basketball. It was a nice April afternoon, and Tone had his DJ equipment out. Lo saw Mack from a distance talking to their cousin Juice. Rob was also on the court dribbling a basketball next to them. He had moved from the Oil to the Gardens as his family grew bigger. He organized a basketball team to play against the Hole and any other team in the city. Lo had interrupted the cousin's conversation as he got near them. First Mack, then Juice greeted him.

"You good, lil bro?"

"Yeah! Just had to ride on them Second Street niggas."

Mack shook his head, then started poking his lil brother's head, scolding him. "Keep your head in them books. Stay out that beef shit."

"I know, but them niggas tried to ride on us, so we had to handle shit." Juice started laughing, but Mack didn't see or hear a joke anywhere in the conversation.

"Just make sure you keep it with your hands and nothing else," Mack said.

"You already know. Y'all balling today?" Juice said yeah, and Mack said no because he had to take his shorty out.

"Oh, you tricking now?" Lo asked. Mack cheesed at his little brother's comment. "How about you treat your brother?"

Mack dipped his hands in his pocket and pulled a knot of money out. He stripped twenty dollars out and passed it to Lo. "Here, and you better not spend it on no weed, nigga."

"Man, I don't smoke. Oh, shit FIVE-O coming up!" Lo alerted them, walking off.

~ ~ ~

After a few hours of shopping with Erica, Mack hopped in his buddy's whip and headed to the Gardens. He met up with Juice, where he continued to talk about his plans. Juice was a year older than Mack and had been selling crack and dope in the Gardens since Rob and Jessica moved there.

Mack told juice that he wanted to take over the Garden's drug trade. And that he wanted his family to control the operation. Juice was down with the plan, he just had to get the rest of his family on board. He had set up a meeting with Rob, Husky, and Vic. Vic was Jessica's brother, who had just came home from serving six years on Riker's Island. He had moved from New York to Allentown to start a new life.

Mack broke the plan down to his family. He wanted each of them to invest what they could, so they could all chip in to buy a brick of coke. He wanted to cook it all up and supply all the young guys from the Gardens with it. He explained that he would find the plug; he just needed a chemist to turn the cocaine into crack. Rob explained that he had a very loyal and reliable buddy for the job. Mack's plan was going smoothly. His family loved the idea. As bad as Mack wanted Ricky to be involved, he just didn't have the time to waste.

Mack had a plug in mind, Diesel. S after the family talk, he drove up to the Hole hoping to run into him. He drove up E. Linden Street and saw that there was no one inside the park. "Strange," he thought to himself. At the top of the hill he made a right on Bradford Street, and he was instantly greeted by the boys in blue.

He slowly drove past them keeping his eyes on the road. He tried to take a glimpse of the person that they had in the back of the cruiser, but he couldn't get a clear view. He didn't want to attract any attention, so he strolled out of the Hole and headed to Erica's. Once he got into the house, he called Big T.

"What's good, boy?" Big T asked.

"I just left the Hole. Saw police had someone. Everyone's good."

"Vice jumped out on Booker. He served vice a dub."

"Damn niggas is thirsty out there. I'm in for the night. Be safe out there."

FIVE

LO WOKE UP EARLY SATURDAY MORNING HOPING

to make it to the Boys and Girls Club on time. He took a shower and got dressed. He put on a pair of Levi jeans and his fresh Polo wifebeater.

"Shit!" he yelled to himself. "Mom ain't wash any clothes."

He checked to see if Mack made it home last night, but he wasn't there. He decided to get a shirt from him since all his were dirty. Lo started searching for a shirt to match his Jordans. Most of the shirts were too big for him. As he picked up one of Mack's Polo flannel shirts, a black film container fell out the pocket and onto the bedroom floor.

The container was all black with a gray lid. It was half the size of a Tylenol bottle. Lo shook the bottle to see if there was anything in it. As he shook it, the sounds of pebbles scattered inside. Lo looked around like someone was in the room with him. He popped the lid off the bottle, and his eyes lit up. Inside was pieces of crack, in all sorts of sizes. Even though he'd been around crack sales all his life, he had never had any of it physically in his possession. He wondered how much of the stuff was in there. He contemplated whether he should take some or put it back where he found it.

He wondered if Mack had each stone counted. It was either now or never, he thought. Knowing that it was wrong on all levels, he took a piece. He wanted to make some fast money too. The piece was a nice size that he took. Lo placed the rock in his pocket, then put the container back in the shirt and closed the dresser drawer. Forgetting about the shirt, he ran out of the room and grabbed a dirty T-shirt out of the hamper and headed to the Hole.

The Boys and Girls Club ended at one. AR, JP, and Lo finished a three-on-three basketball game and headed to the park. Lo was afraid to tell his friend about the work he stole. He had no idea what they would say or think if he did.

He wasn't sure about how he should act if he saw a customer. He had always envisioned himself approaching a customer, real cocky and nonchalant. Then the thought of Mack catching him popped into his head. He would be very disappointed, he thought. As hard as he tried to keep him out of this life, here he was trying to get into it. What did he expect? It had been all around him his whole life. This was how he was raised. Mack should have known that it was just a matter of time before he got his hands on some work.

Lo pushed all those negative thoughts to the back of his head and said to himself, "It's time to get into the drug game."

As the trio entered the park, they were greeted by Blanz and Muzzle, who were shooting hoops, and Frisk, who sat on the park's wall rolling up a Dutch. They joined the shoot around. One by one, old heads and the rest of the young boys showed up to hustle. Lo decided to spin off toward his cousin Kate's house. As he was walking, he ran into Lu Lu, who lived in the Oil also. His brother Melvin was dating Lo's cousin Janet. Lo used this opportunity to get a price on the crack he had in his pocket.

"Lu Lu, what's good?" Lo asked while giving him dap.

"'Bout to head to the circle."

"You alright?"

"Yeah, I'm good, but look what I found in the park," Lo said, pulling out the rock and showing it to Lu Lu. "Can you tell me if this is real or not?"

Lo knew the rock was real; he was playing dumb. Lu Lu opened the sandwich bag and placed the tip of his tongue on the rock. He instantly spit it out.

"Hell yeah, that shit is real," he replied, spitting again. "That shit numbed my tongue Buick as fuck, but that's how you have to check it."

Lo's face was in disgust. "I ain't tasting no crack. How much can I sell it for?"

"It looks like a gram. You can off that for like fifty to a hundred dollars if you want."

"Damn, a little piece of rock is worth that much?" Lo replied in amazement.

Lu Lu explained to Lo the ways to go. He told him to go to the store and buy a razor and showed him how big to chop the chunk.

"Try to make four or five squares. Each square can sell for twenty dollars, or you can sell the whole thing for fifty dollars."

Lo was all ears as Lu Lu broke the game down to him. Chopping grams down to dubs is called a *bust down flow*, and selling grams is called selling weight. Lo was too early in the game to sell weight, so he needed to get a bust down flow. Once he did that, then he could sell weight, he thought to himself. Suddenly another thought crossed his mind. If he moved this work, where would he re-up at? Rock or Diesel? First things first, move what he had, then think about the re-up.

"Good looking, Lu Lu, on schooling me to the game. I'm about to head over to the bodega and cop that razor," Lo said as he stepped off.

He stopped at George's and bought a razor from the cashier. Olga gave him a funny smile as she shook her head. She'd been around long enough to know what he was going to do with the razor.

"Fifty cents," she said as she placed the razor on the counter.

Lo placed a crispy dollar bill on the counter and told Olga he was going to grab an iced tea. Before exiting the store Lo grabbed a straw off the counter. He then grabbed a crate and headed to the woods. There was a spot where him, the young boys, and the old heads would hang out, smoking weed and just talking shit, while the older guys turned their grams into dubs.

There was a shitload of paraphernalia lying around. Dirty razors that had crack residue on them had rusted up from the rain. Stashed under a piece of plywood were the sandwich bags. Lo grabbed a piece of cardboard that lay on the ground and began to go to work. He chopped up four nice size dubs. He calculated eighty dollars, and if he took any shorts, sixty.

~ ~ ~

"Yo!"

"What's up?" a passerby said walking past Lo.

A little past two and the park was flooded. Everybody and their mother were out. The park was full of ballers, hustlers, and spectators. Six different teams lined up to play. There were three teams from the Hole, one from Keck Park (East Side), one from Irving Park, and a team from the Gardens.

Mack, Rob, Juice, Lex, and J.O. were next in line to

play against the Hole's top five, Blanz, Trip, Smooth, Terry, and Muzzle. The away team snuck a win over the home team by two points. The Gardens went on to win the next two games. Mack glanced over at Lo and asked him to run to the store for three gallons of water. Lo picked up a stolen bike and headed to the bodega. He blew past the parked cars hopping on and off curbs like he was a professional biker.

Two seconds later he sped into a huge parking lot then came to a halt in the front of George's. As he exited the store, he spotted Burnt-Face Bill. They called him that because he had a big red birthmark on the left side of his face. Burnt-Face Bill was a regular fiend from the Hole. He turned and faced Lo as he shouted his name.

"What's going on?" Lo asked.

"Nothing much. Let me ask you something," he replied. "You holding?"

It was Lo's first encounter with a fiend. He was nervous as fuck too. He also knew that once he made this sale, given another opportunity, Burnt-Face Bill would be coming back for more.

"Yeah, I'm good. What you need?"

"I got forty."

Lo pulled out two dubs from his pocket and placed them in Bill's hand. He passed Lo the forty dollars and glanced at the product. He then placed the dubs into his mouth and walked away. Cha-ching was the sound going off in Lo's head. He jumped back on the stolen bike with a smile on his face, trying to balance the lopsided bike. After making it back to the park, Lo dropped off the water to Kamikaze, who was security for the park and rode around searching for fiends.

"Five-O going up," yelled Lo from Carlisle Street to the park, giving everyone a heads-up. He popped the two dubs in his mouth and rode to the corner of East Turner Street. He waited there until he witnessed the police cruiser leaving the Hole. Because Lo was so young, the police paid him no mind and just drove right by the young hustler.

After the games were over, niggas from the Gardens and the Hole stuck around smoking, drinking and gossiping about the games. The Gardens ran the courts undefeated. As he spotted Diesel coming out of his mother's projects, he jumped off the wall and headed in his direction.

"Diesel, what's good? You came out here to ball?"

Mack knew that he didn't ball. Last summer Diesel got into a motorcycle accident, after he just purchased a new Suzuki 900. The doctors had to reconstruct his leg, which left him disabled and with a permanent boot and limp. Diesel laughed.

"Nah youngin'. Everything good though?"

"Well, I've been trying to holla at you, but everyone keeps giving me the runaround." Diesel already knew what he was trying to holla at him about, but he played possum to see if he would be straightforward.

"What did you want to holla at me about?"

"You know. I need that raw, but I need a good number. What they looking like?"

Diesel didn't look surprised. Every now and then a pack pusher grew to be a weight pusher if they were smart enough to figure the game out. "Don't you run for Big T?" Diesel asked.

"I did. Now I'm about to do my own thing, in my own spot. Big T was a boost, but now I'm on to bigger things, if you know what I mean. I was just a nigga chasing a dream. Now I need your help to make that dream a reality."

"I feel you, youngin. What you looking for?" Mack asked him what the numbers looked like, and he told him that it depended. It seemed like the conversation was going nowhere and neither wanted to budge. Mack knew this was his only chance to impress Diesel.

"I need a half a man, but if the price is right then, I'ma want the whole thing."

Diesel's eyes widened. "Youngin, that's a lot of cash. You sure you can cover that tab?"

"I wouldn't be asking. You trying to fuck with me or not?" he replied with cockiness in his voice.

"Hold up," Diesel said as he headed back into his mom's house. Two minutes later he came out with a white piece of paper in his hand.

"Here!" He passed the paper to Mack. "Here's my number and the price on what you're looking for. Don't give my number to anyone or the price I'm throwing at you. And when you're ready, holla at me." Mack looked into Diesel's eyes after glancing at the number.

"I'll holla in a few days." He smiled as he gave Diesel dap and walked back to the park.

He finally was about to get the break he always wanted. A connect with raw work at a good price. He didn't need his family to chip in; he could cover the tab by himself. His joy turned into anger as he thought about Big T and Zeus overcharging him. The only difference was that Mack understood the game, and at this moment, things were about to change.

SIX

MEANWHILE, WHILE MACK HAD BEEN CHASING down connects, Ricky had been flaunting his earnings around Big Poppa and his crew. Big Poppa's spot was located on Ninth and Chew Street, a half a block away from Rico's barbershop. During Zeus's surveillance on Rico's runners, he'd noticed that every Saturday Rico collected his weekly rent from his barbers and his workers. Zeus had informed Mack and Ricky about this because he had thoughts of running in the shop, but he noticed that Rico stayed with bodyguards.

Rico pulled up in his electric blue Range Rover driven by his bodyguard. He hopped out the passenger side and scanned the streets. He locked eyes on Big Poppa and his crew. Word was out that Zeus had robbed him. Since the robbery, Ricky had been flossing. He spent twelve hundred dollars on three Coogi sweaters, white Air Forces to match the snow-white sweater, a pair of white-and-red Air Forces to match the other blood-red sweater, and the exclusive six hundred-dollar black Jordan Sevens. Last but not least, he copped a 14-karat-gold Cuban link chain with a solid Jesus piece medallion.

Around six thirty Rico was escorted out the barbershop with his bodyguards at his hip. As they departed from the parking space, the driver drove less than five miles an hour past Big Poppa's house. Rico gave them all a cold stare, but locked eyes with Ricky. He locked eyes with the boss and placed his hand on his hip where his weapon sat.

Ricky was no chump. He stayed on point and strapped. He grilled the drug lord and didn't blink once. If looks could kill, they both would be dead. Ricky got hype as his blood started to boil inside his skin, then yelled out to him.

"What the fuck you looking at?" He raised his left

hand.

"Chill, nigga. You tripping. He's been grilling us since he got robbed," Big Poppa said. "Don't worry about him or anyone else."

"Fuck that nigga. I'll lay his ass down if he keeps grilling me. I don't give a fuck if he's being chauffeured around like a boss. He ain't my fucking boss," yelled Ricky.

Big Poppa and his crew just let Ricky talk. They knew he was going overboard with the situation, but they didn't know what Ricky knew. He was responsible for the robbery of Rico's worker, and he was on point. In this game you do dirt, you get dirt. That's what karma's for. He wouldn't get caught slipping.

SEVEN

TWENTY, FORTY, SIXTY, EIGHTY, A HUNDRED. MACK wrapped the stack in a rubber band and placed it on the mountain of money that lay on his bed.

"That's twenty a brick right there," Mack said out loud to himself.

He was about to buy his first brick. He had dreamed about this moment over six months ago when he served his first dub. He was about to go all in. It was all or nothing. He was putting all his cookies in one basket. It was a risky move in the drug game, but if it all went according to plan, the reward would be worth it.

Mack placed the money inside his book bag and put it inside his closet next to the twenty pairs of sneakers that sat on the floor. He dialed up Juice and asked for his location. Juice told him that he was on his way to the south side, and Mack suggested that they meet up at Jessica's.

Mack was crushing it. He was fresh to death as he stepped out of his buddy's car. He attracted a lot of attention from the project girls. He heard the whistles and glanced at the window where they were coming from. He noticed two females laughing.

"Yo, Juice," he said while tapping his arm. "That's Milly and her butt-ass sister Lori. They're church girls. They ain't got no business fucking with us. Her mom would call the police on us and throw them to the devil if they were caught with niggas like us."

"She keeps looking and passing. She looks bad from over here."

"She's bad, but, cuz, you're setting yourself up fucking around with them. Their mom is no joke. They're not even allowed to walk to the store. I tried to holla at her sister Jamie."

"Damn, there's another one?" Mack said, interrupting Juice.

"Yeah, Lori is the oldest, the one to the right. The one on the left is their baby sister Milly. Jamie is the middle one. Mom dukes got wind of me and Milly and shipped her ass to live with her dad. Don't waste your time."

"Yeah, I feel you, cuz, but she's bad. She got all the features I like in a woman. I'ma get her, you'll see."

"Good luck," Juice laughed.

As they continued to talk business, Mack was flirting with Lori. Then his phone went off. Someone left a text message. It was from an unfamiliar number. When he looked at the number again, that's when it dawned on him that it was an encrypted message from Diesel. He immediately cut his conversation short with Juice.

"Yo, cuz, I gotta handle a situation." Juice asked him if he wanted him to tag along for reinforcements. "Nah, I'm good, cuz. Good looking. Gather up the fam and tell them to be ready. Shit 'bout to go down, Nino Brown style." Mack gave Juice dap and told him he loved him. Juice replied the same as the two departed their separate ways.

Mack and Juice were like brothers. The time Juice spent in foster care nearly tore Mack apart. He felt like he had lost his only family. But that time apart just brought them closer together. So Mack made sure that Juice stood by his side as they took care of each other. They were like the dream team.

Mack slid to his crib, grabbed the book bag and headed to the Hole. He parked up and headed to the back of Diesel's mom's crib. He opened the screen door and gave the door the Hole's signature knock.

From inside the house, a female's voice appeared. "Who's there?"

"It's Mack."

Two seconds later, Diesel came to the door. "Come in." He was looking a bit nervous as Mack entered his house. "Follow me. You want something to drink?" he asked as he escorted him to the kitchen. Mack declined the offer, just wanting to get down to business.

There was an awkward moment. This was the first time either of them had done business together. Mack's name in the streets was intimidating. People were told not to trust him, but Diesel took a chance with the young soldier. Mack felt the tension, so he decided to break the ice.

"Shall we get down to business?"

Mack opened up the book bag revealing the $20,000 and placed it on the table. Diesel opened the fridge without saying a word. He slid open one of the lunch meat compartments and pulled out a plastic bag. He placed it on top of the table, opened it, and pulled out the brick. Diesel then grabbed a steak knife out of the kitchen drawer, walked over to the brick and cut a piece of the wrapper into a V shape. A few layers of the wrapper flapped up.

"Here you go, check it out."

Pure crystals of coke sparkled from the taped-up brick. "Pure fish scale," Mack thought. He placed the brick in the book bag and gave Diesel a pound.

"I'll be calling you soon," Mack said. Then he snuck out of the house like a thief in the night. He called Juice's phone.

"Juice, what's good, cuz? Everything in order?"

"You already know. We are all waiting on you!"

"I'm waiting for this, buddy. I'll be up shortly."

~ ~ ~

Twenty minutes later Mack arrived at Jessica's. At the kitchen table sat Rob, Husky, Vic, and Juice. Mack placed his gun on top of the fridge, then placed the book bag on the table. He unzipped the bag and pulled out the brick. He grabbed the razor out of his back pocket and started cutting through the tape. It was wrapped in layers and layers of tape and oil. Once completely uncovered, he spoke up.

"Now this is what you call coke. High-quality fish scale for your nose."

"You don't know what you're talking about," Vic said. Vic was from the Bronx. He swore that all New Yorkers knew everything that there was about the drug game. "That's nothing. Me and my niggas used to rob the Jamaicans for this type of shit."

"Shut the fuck up, nigga," Juice said, cutting him off while inhaling the smoke from the Dutch. They all started laughing at what he said. "You swear you know everything, but don't know shit."

BOOM! BOOM! BOOM!

A hard knock came from the front door. Mack quickly reached for his gun on top of the refrigerator.

"Chill, cuz. It's probably one of my customers. He gonna chef that up for us," said Rob.

Sure, enough, it was him. Rob had the fiend wait in the living room with Jessica until they were ready. Mack started to break down the work into 250 grams. Once all the work was weighed out, he broke the first 250 down into ounces and placed the other three in sandwich bags.

Rob called his fiend into the kitchen and passed him the Pyrex that held the chunky white substance. The buddy grabbed the container, then grabbed a spoon and started smashing the coke into grains of powder. He then weighed out fourteen grams of baking soda and added it into the cocaine. He placed a hot dog pot of water on top of the stove's medium-high fire. Mack was eager to learn the trade of cooking crack, so he watched and memorized the process.

The fiend grabbed a butter knife and started mixing the coke and the bake together. He then turned on the faucet of water to a light pour. He dipped the Pyrex under the water and watered the coke.

"Not too much water, though," the fiend said. "You want to wet it enough so that it looks like pancake batter."

He stirred the coke until it was evenly mixed, then placed the Pyrex into the boiling water. As the water boiled around the Pyrex, fumes started to enter the atmosphere. The wet coke came to a complete cookie as it dried up.

He then explained, "Look, Mack. When it dries up like that, it's not done yet. You gotta let it break down, but from the looks of it, the way it dried up means it's some good quality coke."

Two seconds later the coke started to break down, releasing its oils. Once it completely broke down, the oils filled the water inside the Pyrex. The fiend lifted the Pyrex out of the boiling water and began to whip the coke with the butter knife. It reminded him of butter.

Once he whipped it, he placed the Pyrex under cold running water and watched the coke lock into a solid cookie. Next, he grabbed a paper towel, took the cookie out of the Pyrex and placed it on the paper towel and wrapped it up so it could absorb the water.

Mack was excited and anxious to see how much work came back. After five minutes he unraveled the paper towel and placed the cookie on the scale. The scale's screen showed 38.5, causing Mack to smile. He broke a piece of the cookie off and gave it to the fiend for his expertise. Mack waited in anticipation for the results. He wanted the okay from the fiend before he started the process again. Ten minutes later the fiend returned from the bathroom, eyes wider than a deer caught the headlights.

"What the fuck was that?" the fiend asked with lockjaw.

Mack panicked. "What? Was it garbage?" he asked, at the same time reaching for his phone to call Diesel.

"Fuck no! That's the best shit I've smoked in years."

"On a scale of one to ten, where would you rate it?" asked Husky.

"Twelve, thirteen. Matter of fact, fuck it, that shit is a fifteen. Best shit out here right now."

Dollar signs filled Mack's brain. He knew that this was a good start to his operation. Mack took out another twenty-eight grams that sat on the table and continued the cooking process that he just witnessed. He crushed up the coke into powder, then added fourteen grams of bake, mixed it, then added water. He mixed the water, coke, and bake until it looked like pancake batter, then placed the Pyrex into the boiling water. He watched it dry up and then the oils release. He added cold water to the coke and watched it lock up.

Mack was so into cooking that he didn't notice that Juice and Rob had left to get some forties and more Dutches. Rob popped the case of Heinekens on the kitchen table, and Juice unraveled the Dutch.

"Time to celebrate," Rob yelled as he cracked open a cold Heineken.

"It ain't party time yet. Let me whip the rest of this coke up," Mack stated.

An hour later Mack was finished cooking the first 250 grams. He then broke everyone off with 50 grams a piece. That's not including the extra that came back that he kept for himself. Mack placed the work in separate sandwich bags and tossed them to his family. Then he cleaned up all the paraphernalia lying around.

"Look, fam. From this day forward, it's F.O.E.: Family Over Everything. If it ain't about us, then it don't make sense. We're going to take over this whole fucking city. A hostile takeover. We're putting everyone that wants to work on. Every young boy that wants to be down with the family, will eat. If niggas don't get down, they'll lay down. Simple as that. No one beefs, unless the beef comes to us. Let's try to stay under the radar. Any questions?"

"Nah," they all said simultaneously.

"Now we celebrate," Mack said.

They all had a cypher going on. Two Dutches were in rotation.

When Husky got high, he liked to release his rap skills: "Snow everywhere, feels like I'm in Alaska, money to be made then ya niches coming after. It's the Garden Gorillas and we taking over fasta . . ."

Before Husky could get another word out, everyone started laughing, busting his train of thought. Vic always wanted to get into the music industry. That was his dream, so he taught Husky all he knew about how to rap and write music.

"After a few flips, we should invest in some studio equipment," Mack said. Husky and Vic agreed. A few hours later, after lots of celebrating, Mack's ride arrived. "I'm out, fam. I'll text y'all with the count. It's time to get to work."

He exited the house, and ten minutes later he was dropped off at Erica's crib. During the ride over there, he did his calculations. He texted everyone with the numbers.

EIGHT

AFTER A WEEK OF HUSTLING AND SHOPPING,
Lo headed to school looking fresh. His swag was on point, but his mind was on after school. He needed to re-up to continue to hustle. As he got to school, he immediately ran into Logan. He was on a thousand. His mouth was rambling, but Lo couldn't understand a word he was saying.

"Slow down, bro, what's going on?"

"Those Second Street niggas jumped Mello. When we see them, it's on and popping," Logan yelled.

"How the hell did they catch Mello slipping? Nobody was with him?" Lo asked.

"I don't know. I just got here, and Sandy was filling me in. JP and AR are around the corner looking for them."

"Say no more. It's war."

Lo's blood was boiling as he sat in homeroom. He knew that once that bell rung for first period, he would be running into one of his enemies. By now everyone knew that there was a war going on with the Hole and Second Street. Word got around like they were passing out fliers. Lo was caught in a vision as he played the ass whooping in his head. Then the telephone rang.

"312, Miss Cohen's room. Yes, yes, he's here," Miss Cohen said as her eyes made contact with Lo. "Okay no problem." She ended the call and looked toward Lo. "Mr. Acevedo, the principal wants to speak with you in his office."

The classroom erupted. Lo smirked as he stood to his feet. He already knew what the conversation was going to be about. Middle school principals were like the school police around the way, always searching for information. He knew he was about to be interrogated. He knocked on the principal's door and was told to enter.

"Hey Alonzo. Take a seat. Is it okay if I call you Alonzo or do you prefer Lo?"

"I don't know no Lo, but you can call me Alonzo," Lo said taking a seat in the chair in front of the desk. "So, what is this all about?"

"Come on kid, don't play dumb with me."

"What are you talking about?"

"Everyone in school has been talking about the beef going on between the Hole and Second Street. Do you want to tell me what that's about?"

"What beef? What's the Hole and Second Street?" Lo said, playing dumb.

"Look, Alonzo," the principal said, raising his voice, tired of the games. "We know that Robert and Ronald got into a fight last week. And then you and your buddies assaulted Ronald and his friends that same day."

"Me? Fight? I don't know what you're talking about,"

he stated, cutting the principal off.

"See, all you kids think that we are stupid, but I'm letting you know one thing: if anything happens to an innocent student, you will be suspended for one week. And if it's worse than what's expected, you and your whole crew will be expelled from my school, with the possibility of charges being filed against you."

"That's it?" Lo said with a smile on his face. "Can I go back to class now?"

"Yeah, get the hell out of here. We got our eyes on you, Alonzo." Lo slammed the door as the principal kept talking.

~ ~ ~

Fifth period was almost over and Lo was surprised that he hadn't run into one of the Second Street boys. But that was the last thing on his mind. All he kept thinking about was getting a re-up. The school bell rang, and he exited the classroom and headed in the direction of his locker. He put his books away, grabbed his fitted and slammed his locker door shut. As he got near the end of the hallway, he heard banging and commotion going on. He turned the corner and noticed Logan and AR fighting. They were on top of two dudes, and one of the dudes was going back and forth hitting them both.

Lo came from left field and stole the dude. He stumbled backward, and Lo jumped on him, wailing on his face. The students that were watching were yelling, which caught the teachers' attention.

"The teachers are coming!" someone yelled.

Everyone began scattering like roaches. Lo and his team ran down the stairs and headed out the side of the building. Once they realized they were safe, they stopped and chilled. Logan was out of breath as he bent over trying to mumble words out of his mouth.

"Goooood, good look, Lo. Shit was hard fighting three motherfuckers at once. They were trying to get the best of us until you came."

"What the fuck happened?"

"AR and I were leaving, when we ran into them niggas. So I dropped the one boy and his man sunk me. Then AR jumped on the other dude."

"Then, the nigga you hit was rocking the both of us," AR chimed in, laughing, rubbing his head.

"Until you came," said Logan. "Good look."

"You already know. We ride and die for ours," Lo said. "Shit gonna be turned up tomorrow if we don't get suspended." They all laughed as they walked through the alley. On the way to the Hole, Lo spotted his ex-girlfriend Jenny and her sister Jessica. "Jenny!" Lo yelled.

She didn't turn around, so Logan and AR decided to help him out. "Jeeeeeeennnnnnyyyy!" She turned around this time, looking in their direction. Lo raised his arm, motioning her to wait. She stopped, and the trio jogged up to them.

75

"Damn, girl, you deaf? I been calling you. How are you doing?" Lo asked.

"I'm sorry, Lo. I didn't hear you. I'm good though," Jenny said with a devilish smile on her face. "And you?"

"I'm okay. What are you doing after you go home? You coming out?" She told him that her mom was going to work at four and she didn't know if she would let them come out.

Before Jazzy got into Lo's life, he was fucking with Jenny. He then decided to test his game and dated both of them at the same time. Jazzy caught wind of it and argued with Jenny, but she held it down and denied their relationship. After their talk, Jenny cut ties with Lo and only flirted with him whenever they saw each other.

"So is it cool if I stop over?" Lo asked with his blue puppy dog eyes.

"You know I can't say no to you, Lo. Come over after six."

"Should I come with AR?"

AR used to mess around with Jessica, until one day after school she caught him holding hands with a high school girl. Jessica beat the brakes off the girl and never spoke to him again. Jenny laughed.

"Well it looks like they're okay now. So, yeah, bring him with you."

During the walk home from school to the Hole, Lo and Jenny were kicking it like the good old days. They held hands like if they were a couple. Lo always had a thing for her, but Jazzy stole his heart. He had mixed emotions for them both. He knew if Jazzy found out about their walk, shit would get crazy. Once they reached the Hole, Logan went his way, while Lo and AR walked the girls home.

"I guess this is your stop," Lo said, still holding Jenny's hand.

She stared into his eyes, leaned forward and gave him a soft tap kiss. Lo grabbed her waist and pulled her toward him, sliding his tongue into her mouth. Jenny pulled back as she smiled, teasing him.

"Come back later and we can finish what you started," she told him.

Lo patted her on the ass and smiled. "I'll see you soon." His eyes followed her ass as she walked to her front door.

"Damn, my nigga, you lucky as hell," AR said.

Lo erased Jenny from his mind and got focused as he walked toward the park. He needed to re-up. He scanned the park to see if he saw Rock, but he didn't. He only saw a few old heads sitting around conversing and Logan shooting around on the basketball court.

"Logan, you seen Rock?"

"He just went to his crib like five minutes ago. What you need him for?" Logan asked, confused.

"I just gotta holla at him real quick. I'ma head to the

store. I'll be back in a few minutes." Lo took the long way as he headed to the store. As he hit the yellow poles, he stopped in his tracks. "What's up, bro?" He was surprised to run into Mack.

"You tell me, little bro? I heard you had a little scuffle at school," Mack stated.

"Yeah them Second Street niggas was jumping Logan and AR, so I had to jump in. You know the rules."

"Yeah, no fair ones. I feel you, little bro."

Lo knew from the look in Mack's eyes he wasn't happy about the situation. Then Mack pointed to his head and spoke.

"Keep your mind on them books, bro. Get your education; fuck these streets. Don't get caught up in this shit. It's not for you. I'll turn this city red if something happens to you."

"I got you, bro. I was just protecting myself," Lo replied, trying to minimize the fight.

"Alright, where you going?" Lo told him to the store.

"You got money?"

"Yeah, I have two dollars," he lied.

Mack then dug into his pocket and pulled out a knot of loose bills. "Here's ten dollars. Get you something to eat." Lo grabbed the money and dapped his brother up. Mack kissed him on top of his head and whispered, "Be safe, bro."

Ever since their father went to prison, Mack had been Lo's father figure. Anything that Lo asked for, Mack tried his hardest to provide it. Mack didn't want him following in his or his father's footsteps. He wanted Lo to live a better life than any of them. He would always give him advice telling him to stay in school, and the importance of education, while he did the hard work to take care of their family. He wanted Lo to make their mother proud by graduating and staying out of the drug life. The only problem was, Lo looked up to Mack and wanted to be like him. He had planted a seed, and that seed was about to sprout.

Lo grabbed a turkey and cheese sandwich, a bag of Doritos, and an iced tea and placed it on the counter. He paid for his food and sat on a crate outside the store. As he sat and ate his food, he spotted Rock pulling into the parking lot in his gold Toyota Camry. Through the windshield Lo noticed the fly Puerto Rican that sat in the passenger seat. Rock hopped out of his car and greeted his young boy.

"Damn, who shorty?" Lo asked.

Rock cheesed. "Come on, young boy, you wouldn't know what to do with that. I just met her. She from the city. You alright?"

"Yeah, I'm good. But listen, I've been wanting to holla at you. You got a minute or two?"

"Yeah, let me grab these Dutches real quick."

Lo waited anxiously outside the store. This could be

his shot to pull a plug on his own, but Mack came to his mind. Rock could easily deny him work on the strength of Mack. It was all or nothing. George's metal door opened as Rock slipped out, Dutches and a Mountain Dew in hand.

"What you want to talk about?"

"I need a frizzy."

"You need a what?" Rock asked like he was hearing him wrong. He told Rock he needed a gram again. "I knew I wasn't hearing wrong. Does your brother know you're out here hustling?"

"No, he don't know, and don't tell him either. I'm just out here trying to eat like everyone else."

"I don't know if that's a good thing," Rock said, looking at his Rolex. "You know if Mack finds out I sold you work, it's going to be a problem."

"Come on, Rock. If I don't get it from you, I'll get it from someone else in the park. I'd rather get it off of you. At least I know the shit is real." Lo could see from Rock's facial expression that he didn't want to sell him no work. Not because it was a gram; it was because of Mack. If Mack found out, Rock's family would be getting tailored up for his funeral.

"Hold on," Rock said as he walked over to the passenger side window of his car. He reached in and popped his trunk. He slammed his trunk closed after retrieving something. He walked back to Lo and lifted his hand as to give him dap. When the two hands met, Rock placed a chunk of crack into Lo's hand. Lo placed the chunk into his pocket and put his left hand into his left pocket and pulled out his last forty dollars. "What's that for?"

"For the gram."

Rock laughed. "First things first, if you're trying to get into this game, you need to learn the weight of the drugs first. What I gave you is a bill. Three and a half grams."

"But I only have forty dollars."

"Don't disrespect me, young boy. When I see you, I see myself when I was growing up. I followed all Diesel's moves just like you're following your brother's. Keep the forty dollars and the work. That's on the hood. Start with that and work your way up. Come back to me when you're done, and not for no gram. That'll be hustling backward."

Lo sat there soaking up all the knowledge that was being given to him. He was surprised that Rock was putting him under his wing. Little did Rock know, Lo was eyeing his position. He knew he had to start small, and he planned to start with his crew.

"Good look, Rock. Give me a couple of days. I'll be back and I'll be coming correct."

"Alright, be a safe young boy. Listen, if any fiends come around asking for me, tell them that you're my little brother and serve them."

"Say no more. I'll make sure I'll take care of them," Lo

said. He gave Rock a pound and quickly walked into George's and grabbed a box of sandwich bags and a razor. He exited the store and walked directly into the woods.

NINE

(OVER ON THE NORTH SIDE)

"Damn, young boy. I've been looking for you. You trying to go eat?"

"You treating?" Ricky asked as he jogged toward the big white truck, holding on to his gun strapped to his waist.

"You strapped?"

"Always."

"Youngin, stay ready for war," Zeus said as Ricky jumped into the truck. "You heard of that new spot near Dorney Carrabas? We gonna hit that up."

"Say no more," Ricky replied.

Thirty minutes later, after they exited the restaurant, Zeus lit up a blunt. Ricky was still in his feelings about

Rico. "Why the boy Rico stay grilling me? Do them niggas know it was us that got him?"

"Nah, that don't have a clue. I did my homework and shit won't get back to us. They assuming I was involved, but like I said, assuming. What's up with Mack? He's been dodging me."

"I haven't seen him. He's been on the south side with his family, but let's get back to Rico. Niggas was mean mugging me, so I grabbed my joint letting him know that I stay strapped."

"Ricky, you shot out. Don't worry, we good. Ain't nobody touching my main man, NOBODY!" Zeus yelled. "I got you. You just paranoid."

"Nah, I ain't paranoid, I'm just on point, and I won't get caught slipping. Any more licks?"

"Speaking of that. I've been scheming on this cat from Easton. He from the Terrace Projects. He runs with the Bloods. He's waiting on this shipment, five bricks and fifty pounds."

Ricky's eyes lit up like a Christmas tree.

"I might need my team to ride with me on this one if we gotta go to Easton."

"Team? Who you speaking of? You know the more people involved, the more we gotta worry about them running their mouths. Plus, less profit."

"Me, you, Mack, Big Poppa, and Pretty Boy."

For the first time Ricky was using his head. He wasn't down with the scheme one bit. "I'll think about it. I gotta holla at Mack first."

"We don't really need Mack unless we go to Easton. I'm trying to bring him down here. That way it will be just you and I, with Pretty Boy and Big Poppa on guard. He'll be out of his comfort zone, and you know, LIGHTS OUT!"

"You plan on offing dude?"

"If we get him, he's capable of starting a war. So we

might as well."

"When is this going down?"

"Next week if everything goes according to plan."

"You know I'm riding. I gotta get this money."

"I knew you would," Zeus said.

The setup was going according to his plan. Ricky was jeopardizing his hit on Rico by flossing too much. As Ricky was walking, he noticed Rico's Range Rover parked outside the barbershop, so he decided to test the waters. As he swung the door open, he noticed Rico spin around in his direction.

"Anyone cutting?" Ricky asked.

Before Rico could speak, one of his barbers spoke up. "Yes, take a seat." As he turned his chair toward Ricky to sit down, Rico just stared into Ricky's eyes with a look of disrespect.

Ricky was just like Mack; they got a rush when they

went behind enemy lines. They liked to check their enemy's temperature by going into their comfort zone. Rico got up out of the chair and walked to his office, blood boiling in his body. He knew the art of war and he didn't want to expose his cards. He sat in his office and watched Ricky through his two-way window.

Ricky asked for a shapeup and demanded the barber not to push his hairline back. Once the barber placed the cape over Ricky's chest, he pulled out his gun and placed it on his lap. Ten minutes later, Ricky stepped out of the barbershop and walked toward Big Poppa's house laughing to himself as he pictured Rico's facial expression when he entered his business.

He then took a look back, checking his surroundings, and noticed Rico standing outside his shop staring at him. Ricky stopped in full stride, thinking about turning back, but kept moving.

"I'ma catch him slipping. You'll see," Ricky thought to himself.

TEN

"LOGAN, YOU SEEN AR?" LO ASKED.

"He was just looking for you. He was walking toward the lollipop."

"Shit, he left me. We 'bout to go chill with Jenny and Jessica."

"Word. I'm 'bout to go to the Boys Club. Let's swing by," Logan said.

As Lo and Logan got to the end of Logan's Row, they spotted AR standing on the corner of Turner and Carlisle. Lo yelled his name as they jogged toward him.

"Damn, Lo, where have you been? I was looking all over for you," AR said.

"I went to the Bodega and ate, then I was at Kate's house," he lied.

Logan dipped behind the row houses toward the Boys

Club, while Lo and AR walked to the front of Jenny's house. The screen door was open, as someone was standing in the doorway. As they got closer, they noticed that it was Jessica.

"What's up, baby?" AR said to Jessica. She didn't reply. They could tell that she was playing hard to get. She then rolled her eyes and looked at Lo.

"Jenny's upstairs. Hold on, let me get her."

She closed the screen door and yelled up to Jenny. Lo's heart started racing as he heard footsteps coming down the stairs. Jenny opened the door with the biggest smile.

"Hey, Lo. It took you long enough."

"I'm sorry, ma. I had to take care of something real quick."

"Hi, Jenny. Is Jessica coming back out?" AR asked.

"You know Jessica, she's a bitch. Just go inside,"

Jenny said.

AR didn't hesitate. He swung the door open almost hitting Jenny on her leg. He apologized, and they all laughed as he entered the house. Jenny grabbed Lo's hands and pulled him closer to her. Lo smelled the sweet aroma of wintergreen gum coming from her breath.

"You're not going to get into any trouble if Jazzy sees you here, right?"

"Come on, Jenny, I don't have a girlfriend," Lo said, lying. Inside his mind he knew that if Jazzy found out, all hell would break loose. Lo and Jazzy had what you call an on-and-off relationship. One minute they were together, the next they weren't. This was one of those off days.

"Well I hope not. You know I'm not with the drama."

"We cool, ma," Lo said as he leaned in and kissed her.

Jenny had the softest lips that Lo has kissed in his

young life. He loved hanging out with Jenny. The two of them had an amazing vibe, and she was really mature for her age. They spoke about high school and their plans for when they got older. Jenny wanted to follow her mother's footsteps and become a nurse. She already had plans of signing up for vo-tech and taking CNA classes when she there. Lo was flirting with her and told her how beautiful she would look in scrubs. Then she hit him with the question.

"So, what are your plans, Lo? What do you want to be?"

For a second Lo was stuck. He had never thought about the road ahead. When he was younger, he used to tell his father that he wanted to become a lawyer, but that dream slowly faded away as he got older. Lo thought to himself, but the only thing he could think about was hustling. He knew he couldn't tell her that though.

"Sooooo?" Jenny said, snapping him out of his thoughts. "What do you want to be?"

"I don't know yet, ma. I really haven't thought that far into the future yet. Whatever I do though, I want to be rich."

"It's okay, pa, you'll figure it out," she told him as she placed another kiss on his lips.

After a few hours with Jenny, the streetlights came on. Jenny sat between his legs as he hugged her from behind. Lo knew that he had missed a whole day from trapping because he was chilling with Jenny, but he was enjoying the moment.

"Ma, can you get AR and tell him that I'm about to be out," Lo whispered in her ear.

She quickly grabbed Lo and held his arms tight. "Noooooo. I don't want you to leave. My mother isn't coming home for a couple more hours."

"I know, ma. I just don't want it to get too late. You know I gotta walk home," he said, giving her the sad puppy look. From the corner of his eye, he saw a fiend coming up the Oil steps. "Yooooo!" Lo yelled, raising his arm.

Jenny was confused as she released her hug from Lo. She had no idea what he was doing as he stood up from his position. Jenny was looking at Lo like he had lost his mind as he jogged toward the unknown man.

"What's good? What you need?"

"I'm going to see Rock," the fiend said.

"I'm Rock's little brother. I can take care of you."

The fiend didn't bother to ask any questions. Lo figured he saw some type of resemblance. "I only got one fifty. Hook me up."

Lo's eyes lit up. He was in shock but played it smooth. He pulled his Garcia Vega tube from his pocket and placed nine chunky dubs in his hand. "Here, and here's an extra dub on the house. I go by Lo, Rock's little brother."

He was so caught up in the streets that he had forgot that Jenny was watching the entire transaction. He placed the money in his pocket before he turned around to face her. As he got closer to her, he could see the shock and disappointment in her face.

"What was that all about?" Jenny asked.

"What do you mean?"

"Lo, I'm not stupid. Are you selling drugs?"

"Um, something like that."

Jenny's eyes got watery as she looked him in the eyes. She knew that he was lost in the streets, but was hoping that she could change him.

"I just don't want nothing bad to happen to you. I don't want to see you getting locked up for chasing dirty money."

"It's okay, ma. Do I look old enough to sell drugs? No," Lo said, answering his own question. "So the police won't be worried about me. Plus, I only deal with the regular customers that have been coming for years."

"Okay, Lo. Just make sure and be careful."

That was the difference between Jenny and Jazzy. Jenny was a real sweetheart and let her emotions be seen. Unlike Jazzy. She would never show her emotions, and she was hard to read.

"So, since you made some money, I can call you an Uber and you can stay a little longer until they come."

Lo smiled. At thirteen years old, she knew how to take care of a man. Twenty minutes later the Uber showed up for him. He gave Jenny a long kiss goodbye. He told her to tell AR that he went home and that he would see him tomorrow. He gave her a few more kisses before he headed to the awaiting car. As the car drove off, he looked out the rearview window and noticed that Jenny was still on her porch watching the Uber the entire time. He knew that he had a keeper in Jenny. He smiled, and then his smile turned to a frown as he thought about Jazzy. She

was also a keeper. The entire ride home, he fought about

both girls. He was torn between the two women. What's

the worst that could happen?

ELEVEN

A WEEK WENT BY AND NO ONE HAD HEARD

from Ricky. This was unusual and something that he didn't do, thought Mack. At least twice a week Ricky would check in with Mack no matter what. Last time he heard from Ricky was about a week ago when they spoke about Zeus and his new heist. Mack didn't like the plan. He told him that he thought the plan was shady and a setup. Ricky didn't agree with his thoughts, and Mack felt that was why Ricky was being distant. Mack didn't need to rob anyone anymore; he was where he wanted to be. He had just linked up with Diesel and started his operation on the south side.

Mack was frustrated that Ricky hadn't called him, so he decided to stroll to his house. He pulled up in front of the house located on Seventh Street. The house had piles of garbage bags sitting on the porch. There was a loveseat centered with an ashtray on one of its arms. On the wooden door a sign hung, which read, God Protect Us from All Evil. Mack chuckled as he read the sign. He didn't believe in God. He lost all faith when his grandmother Julia died. He prayed and prayed for God to heal her, hoping he'd answer his prayers, and when he didn't and she passed away, Mack had a grudge against his maker.

"The only thing that's going to protect me is this cannon on my hip," he mumbled to himself.

Ricky's mother was heavy on religion. She believed that God would take care of all her needs. She attended church four times a week, not counting Sundays. Mack heard footsteps running around from outside where he stood. Ricky's mom, Isabel, had three other small children: Tina, Angel, and Sammy. After five minutes of knocking, the door opened.

"Hi, Mack!" Isabel yelled in glee. "How have you

been? It's been a long time that I haven't seen you. You're getting all big and stuff."

"I've been good. Just drinking my milk and working out. Have you seen Ricky?"

"Boy, I haven't seen Ricky in months. He comes in when I'm at work or at church. He showers and changes clothes, then he's gone. He's no help with the kids, and he doesn't even bother to help pay the bills. Our cable just got turned off, next will be the lights, and my job is going under. I pray and pray, and nothing seems to work. I don't know what to do."

Mack knew that Ricky was lying when he said that he had to help his mom with the bills and couldn't invest. Isabel was like Mack's second mother. Whenever he needed a place to crash or eat, her doors were always open. He put his hand in his pocket.

"Here's two stacks, ma. Take care of whatever you have to. Pay the bills in advance and go food shopping. I will send someone over here to clean up the porch for you, and when you see Ricky, tell him that I'm looking for him. If you need anything else don't hesitate to call or text my phone."

"Thank you so much, baby." Isabel gave him a big hug. "I knew the Lord would answer my prayers. God bless you, Mack."

Mack gave her a kiss on the cheek and walked off the porch, heading toward his buddy's car. His blood was boiling.

"Why the fuck would he lie and not contribute to help his family?" he thought to himself.

Mack knew where to look next. He jumped into the car and pulled off, tires screeching. He hit every corner at high speed, nearly tipping over the car. He pulled in front of Big Poppa's house and jumped out of the whip, leaving the car double-parked. Pretty Boy was the only one out.

"Yo, where Ricky at?"

"He just left with Zeus and Big Poppa to grab some toys."

"Grab toys for what?" Mack yelled. He already knew what the toys were for, so he tried to get more info out of Pretty Boy.

"Ricky didn't tell you about the Easton nigga?"

"Yeah, he had run some bullshit by me, but he never got back to me. Why, shit 'bout to go down?"

"Yeah, Zeus supposed to link up with the nigga this evening at the park."

"Which park?"

"Jordan Park, but you know what the plan is," Pretty Boy said, laughing as if death was a joke.

"Fuck that plan," he thought. "Zeus is going to get Ricky killed, and he's so stupid and too damn blind to see the shit. He needed to bet Ricky out of that situation before things got out of hand and they brought heat to the

Gardens.

"Tell Ricky to holla at me as soon as they get back and tell him I said before the lick."

"Be easy, playboy, he's in good hands," Pretty Boy said as he winked at Mack.

Mack tensed up. He placed his hand on his hip reaching for his toy. He hesitated as he caught himself. It was broad daylight, too many witnesses. He wanted to blow Pretty Boy's face right off his neck after his slick-ass comment.

"Yeah, you right, he's in good hands. Tell him to call me ASAP."

At that moment, Zeus and his team were starting to rub Mack the wrong way. He already had his mind set that Pretty Boy would be the first nigga to get it. He jumped in his buddy's whip and drove off. He pulled out his gun and started speaking to it like an insane person.

"It's okay, baby, you'll get to taste his blood sooner or

later. There is a time and place for everything. Every dog has its day."

~ ~ ~

(4 HOURS LATER)

You could smell death in the air. Mack impatiently waited on Ricky's call that never came. He felt that something was extremely wrong. The sun was going down and that meant that the drop was about to go down. Mack drove through the Gardens and noticed Juice posted up at the mailbox. Mack pulled up and lowered the passenger window.

"What's good, cuzzo? Everything good?" Juice said, walking toward the car.

"Nah, the nigga Ricky is on some nut shit. Zeus got him making flunky moves, and they about to do this lick and planning on bodying this nigga."

"I told you before, cuz, he's a follower, not a leader. You need to cut those ties before shit hits the fan and he brings us all down with him."

"I feel you, cuz. Hop in, let's take this ride. I have a bad feeling about this. You holding?"

"When ain't I?" Juice said, holding up his shirt.

Inside the car was silent until they exited the Gardens. "So, who's the vic?" asked Juice.

"Some blood nigga from Easton. Suppose to be some bricks and bud."

"Damn, niggas got work like that out there?"

"I guess, but Zeus thinks that he can rob every and anyone. Sooner or later shit's going to catch up to him."

"Yeah, I feel you. Karma's a motherfucker. Where we heading?" Mack told him Jordan Park. "That's where the drop is at?"

"Yeah. I ran up on one of Zeus's workers and he dropped dime. Talking about Ricky's in good hands. Shit seems funny to me. Like why didn't he ride? I'll kill one of them niggas if they set Ricky up."

Juice didn't bother to chime in on that. He felt his own way about Ricky. He didn't need to express himself anymore. As the two got closer to the park, from a distance they noticed the red-and-blue lights flashing. Their first thoughts were someone got bodied. Mack made a quick detour up Sixth Street and headed toward Big Poppa's house. Mack circled the spot three times, and no sign of Zeus or his crew. Mack drove past Isabel's house. It was pitch black. His mind was racing.

He didn't know what to think. Did his right-hand man body somebody in the park, or was he the victim of a homicide? It seemed like a brick was on top of the gas pedal as Mack sped through the city. He headed to his safe zone, the Gardens. He pulled up to the mailboxes and parked up. A group of the Gorilla soldiers was outside. As Mack and Juice jumped out, they immediately greeted everyone. Mack was so caught up in his thoughts, that he was surprised by the new face that he was about to dap up.

His face was unfamiliar. Mack didn't miss a beat as their eyes met and their hands touched.

"Mack," Mack said as he shook the unfamiliar teenager's hand, greeting him.

"Junito," the young teen responded. "I've heard all about you."

"Is that right?" Mack said as he glanced at Juice. "That must not be a good thing you heard then."

"Nah, all good things. Your family told me what you have been trying to do for the hood. All for a good cause, so I'm just letting you know it's all love this way."

"No doubt," Mack said. The cousins walked off, heading toward Jessica's house.

"Who's that kid Junito?" Mack asked.

"My bad, cuz. I forgot to put you on. Junito is one of the realest young boys out here. He's not the type of kid that likes to hustle. He's more into putting in that work. And with all the shit going on with Ricky and Zeus, you need a nigga like that around you at all times. Especially when handling business. He should be your muscle."

Mack thought to himself that from the looks of Junito, he was a little husky for his age. "Does he got a box game?"

"Young boy is nice with his hands. He be knocking out old heads twice his size. Last New Year's, he knocked out old head John from up the block."

"That big fat muthafucka?"

"Yup. He caught him rapping to this young girl near the center. John was out for a good five minutes, and old head was a boxer in his early years. I guess he didn't see that hook coming."

"Okay, okay. I like to hear that. I'ma have to keep him around me. We gonna see what he's about soon because the way it's looking, it's about to be war out here."

~ ~ ~

"Hello, hello," Mack said as he answered his phone. Before the person on the other end could finish another word, Mack cut them off. "Where the fuck are you? I've been looking for you all fucking day." There was a pause. "Look Mack, I can't talk. Meet me at the spot. Hurry up and come fast!"

Mack was confused. He started pacing, then began to panic. "Oh shit, the spot," he said out loud. He knew that couldn't be good. He hopped in the whip and flew to the spot. He gunned the pedal to the max. All he was concerned about was the phone call he had received. He was contemplating each muthafucka he was going to kill. He wanted to start with the head of the snake.

Mack also wanted the snake to suffer, so he thought about starting with the flunkies. He started banging on the steering wheel, screaming, "I'm gonna kill them muthafuckas!"

He ran a red light, then another. He parked a block away from his spot just in case he was being followed. He wasn't scared; he was cautious. He waited a minute before he exited the car. Mack slid out of the whip and dipped into the alley. He reached his spot, heart racing, not knowing what to expect when he entered the dark apartment. The key was already drawn. He slowly slid the key into the keyhole, then turned the knob. The door became ajar. There was no sound from the empty apartment.

Mack pulled his gun out from his waistband before he entered. There wasn't a single soul in the apartment from what he could see. He found a corner that was angled directly to the door. He crouched down in a shooter's position, kneeling on one knee. He aimed the gun at the door waist-high, waiting for an intruder to enter.

"If the caller ain't the next person walking through that door, they getting stretched," he mumbled to himself as he continued to watch for any movements. He had a gas container full of gas in the trunk of his car just in case shit went sour.

He was planning on torching the place. Mack played the streets like a game of chess; he was always two moves ahead of his opponents. And if this meeting was a setup, Mack was prepared for plan B. He heard footsteps coming near the apartment door. There was heavy breathing.

The sounds of a man in serious pain could be heard. Mack focused on the door and its knob. The knob giggled as the unknown person tried to open the door. Next, he heard the sound of a set of keys fumbling around and being placed into the keyhole. Mack gripped his gun even tighter, finger on the trigger, ready to let the cannon bark.

The doorknob turned, then cracked open. Mack remained focused. The intruder entered the apartment, and Mack recognized the familiar face. Still in the shooter's stance, the intruder jumped at the drawn gun.

"MACK IT'S ME DON'T SHOOT. I'VE BEEN SHOT!"

TWELVE

SCHOOL WAS NOW OUT. THE ENTIRE WEEK, THE
talk of the beef between the Hole and Second Street was
popular. On the low, Frisk and MC squashed the beef. Lo
had spoken to Frisk and told him it was best if they
squashed. The beef would only escalate since neither
side would back down. Lo also knew from Mack's
preaching, you can't beef and get money at the same
time. Besides the talk about the fights, word spread like
wildfire that Lo was seeing Jenny. He had only chilled with
her a few times, but nothing went farther than her house.
Someone was hating.

Lo met with the young gangstas on Chestnut. Upon
his arrival he noticed that Jazzy and Jenny were
speaking. Lo already knew what that conversation
consisted of. He remained calm as he walked up to Jazzy
and kissed her on her lips. He knew the game, and he

played it smoothly. Plus, he knew that Jenny wouldn't expose their relationship.

After Jazzy let her voice be heard, she apologized. "I'm sorry, Jenny. You know how people like to talk shit."

"It's okay, girl. Lo and I are old news. Besides, ya look so cute together."

Jazzy held on to Lo's arm as they walked away from Jenny. "What are you doing today?" Lo asked Jazzy as they walked through the alleyway.

"I'm going to Kim and Sandy's house until the Boys and Girls Club opens. We gonna practice some dances, and you?"

"I'm going to see if I can get a ride to the mall so I can buy me some clothes for school."

"Are you going to buy me something?"

"I'll see," he replied. Lo already had it in his mind that he was going to surprise her with a gift. He knew she was infatuated with Mickey and Minnie Mouse, so a shirt was on his mind.

"Did your mom give you money?" Jazzy asked.

Lo was stuck. He didn't expect her to question his finances. He hesitated. "Umm, umm, something like that."

"What do you mean something like that?"

"Huh?"

"Don't huh me. I hope you're not out there selling drugs."

"I gotta make money somehow," Lo said on the defensive. "Besides, baby, I'm cool. I only serve the people I know."

Jazzy gave him a dirty look as she tried to release her hand from his. Lo held on to her hand tightly as he pleaded with her. "Trust me, baby, I'm good."

"Just be careful. I just don't want you getting locked up on me. I love you too much."

At that moment all the guilt in the world entered Lo's body. All the dirt he did to her while they were together crept up on him, and it hit him hard. That was the first time Jazzy had showed her true feelings for him. The thought of chilling with Jenny and kissing Sandy stopped him in his tracks. He hugged Jazzy and looked into her beautiful brown eyes.

"I know that you don't want me to go to jail, and I don't want to either, but this is only temporary. I'll be careful, and I love you too." Then he kissed her softly. A shiver went down his spine; he didn't want to let her go.

"Awwww," a female's voice came from behind them. The young couple looked back and saw Kim holding hands with Juan Pepe and Sandy mean grilling Lo, Logan, AR, Frisk, and Mello. "Y'all look so cute together."

They all trotted across the bridge heading to their safe grounds. Lo walked Jazzy to the park and gave her a kiss. "I'll see you later."

~ ~ ~

Lo stood on the court splashing a three, while Logan passed the ball back to him after every shot. They were playing layups. The park was dead for some reason, but they didn't care. In fact, that's how they liked it to be. There were no hustlers out, and not a single fiend came through. AR showed up and gave them a pound, then joined in on the festivities.

"Y'all trying to hit the store," Lo asked once they started to chill.

"I ain't got no money," Logan and AR said at the same time.

"It's cool, I got y'all. Let's take this walk."

After Logan ran his basketball to the crib, the trio walked over to George's. "Grab whatever you want. It's all on me," Lo said.

"Anything?"

"Anything," Lo replied. It only took three days to get rid of the work Rock gave him. With a little over three hundred dollars in his pockets, he felt like he was on top of the world. They each ordered sandwiches, Logan grabbed a bag of chips and a juice, AR grabbed a krimpet and a juice, while Lo grabbed his usual iced tea and Doritos.

"Yo, Jenny kept it real today when Jazzy approached her. I gotta give it to her, she didn't flinch. I owe her big time."

"Yeah, she a rider."

As Lo pulled out his money to pay for the food and drinks, AR's and Logan's eyes widened. They were surprised that he had so much money.

"Let me find out that you're hustling," Logan said, looking at the stack of bills in his hand.

"What you mean?" asked Lo.

"You either dipped in Mack's stash or you're hustling.

Which one is it?"

"I didn't rob Mack. I tried to buy a grizzly off of Rock, and he threw me a ball."

"You crazy!"

"You holding out on us?" AR finally chimed in and said.

"Nah, bro, I didn't say shit because I didn't want Mack finding out."

"I heard he got the Gardens on smash. He's not worried about you. You gotta put me on. I'm trying to make some money too."

"Yeah, Mack is doing his thing up there. I'm just testing the waters, but I got you."

Logan chimed in. "Man, I ain't no drug dealer, leave me out."

Lo and AR laughed as they left the store. As they headed toward the park, a blue Chevy Cavalier slowly drifted up East Linden Street. Lo noticed the driver staring in his direction. He recognized the glasses she was wearing. They were brown with clear lenses. He remembered the odd color the day she was parked up at the yellow poles speaking to Blanz. She was a customer. Lo threw up his right hand trying to flag her down. She stopped and rolled her window down.

"Hey, Rock, are you holding?"

Logan and AR looked around to see if Rock was near. Lo knew that she was talking to him. Before Logan and AR caught on, Lo spoke. "Yeah, hold up." Lo jogged to the passenger door and hopped in. The customer drove up the hill and made a right on Bradford and let Lo out at the top of the park, where Logan and AR waited. From a distance Lo could hear the two speaking.

"We gotta get this money. All we gotta do is sit here and watch who the old heads serve, and when they are not around, we serve them like Lo does."

"Yup. That's what I do," Lo said, interrupting them.

"Plus, the fiends think that I am Rock or his little brother,

so I run with it."

"How much did she want?"

"A thirty. All I had was two dubs left, so I hooked her

up."

"Fuck that, I ain't giving up no shorts."

"See, that's where you go wrong. We're young. In

order for us to make money and for fiends come to us, we

gotta take whatever comes our way. We need them, so

I'm taking them all, five, ten, even seventeen." Lo could

see that AR was determined to hustle. He could use the

help also.

"How much you made?"

"With shorts and all, a little over three hundred this

week."

"Three hundred?" AR's eyes lit up. "You have to put

me on."

"I got you. Don't worry," Lo said as they finished their dinner and headed to the Boys and Girls Club.

After running a game of basketball, Lo dipped into the TV room. It was isolated from everybody. He just wanted to get his thoughts together. The room was filled with all the board games you could find. At the end of the room, in the corner of the wall, sat an old twenty-inch TV. It was used for watching sports games or if one of the older kids brought in their game system. The room was completely silent. He was playing chess again in his mind. He tried to calculate his next move. His train of thought was interrupted by a soft kiss on his neck, causing his pipe to pump.

"Did I scare you?" Jazzy asked as she sat on his lap.

"No!"

"I see that you're excited to see me," she replied, feeling on his erection. Lo smiled.

"What's wrong? Why are you sitting in here all alone?"

"I'm just getting my thoughts together," Lo said as he rubbed her ass. "What you do at Kim's?"

"We practiced our dance. You want me to show you what we learned?"

Before Lo could answer yes, she started grinding on him. Her body moved slowly on his pipe as she kissed his lips. She moved her hips back and forth. Lo grabbed her ass as their tongues fought. He pulled her closer as she continued to rock back and forth on his lap.

THIRTEEN

RICKY WAS RELEASED FROM THE HOSPITAL

after being shot twice. One in the leg and another in the stomach. Luckily no organs or main arteries were hit, or he wouldn't have survived. Through the entire surgery and time in the hospital, Mack was by his side. Each time detectives came to the hospital, trying to get him to cooperate, Mack would be home showering. Isabel cried as Mack escorted Ricky out of the hospital in a wheelchair. She ran to him pleading.

"Please, papi, stay out of the streets. Look what they done to you!"

Ricky ignored her pleas. He had other plans. His plan was to find out from Zeus who was responsible for shooting him. The ride home was quiet. Through the music, all you could hear was Isabel sobbing. Mack glanced at Ricky a few times through the mirror. Mack knew where his mind was at, and he didn't want to interrupt. Ricky was plotting murder.

Mack pulled up to Isabel's house. He grabbed the cane the hospital provided for Ricky and helped him out of the car. Ricky stood up in pain as he tried to balance himself without the cane. Mack held on to Ricky until he balanced himself using the cane. Mack guided him into the house and up the stairs to his bedroom.

"Take a shower and get some rest. I'll be back."

"I just want to kill them niggas that shot me."

"I know you do, and so do I, but you need to heal up first before we can move. Get up out of these hospital clothes and shower up. Call me if you need anything, I'll be around."

Mack left Ricky's crib and hopped in his whip. As he drove down the road, he ran Ricky's story through his head.

Ricky had told him, "Zeus parked in the parking lot

and hopped out. I hid in the dark and watched him jump on his jack. Two minutes later the Easton dude pulled up. Zeus then jumped in the passenger seat and made the transaction. Our plan was, once he hopped out, I'd ambush the dude.

"Once he hopped out and made his way into his car, I made my move out of the dark. I put the gun on dude and tried to grab the money, then a shot rang out. Dude was on point. He shot me in the stomach, and I shot back. I'm not sure if I hit him, but he reversed out, and I heard more shots. That's when I got hit in the leg. I couldn't see where the shots came from, so I ran for cover."

Why didn't Zeus just hold him at gunpoint while Ricky smoked him? The situation didn't seem right at all. In Mack's eyes, it was a setup. He was trying to get Ricky killed, but why take him to Jordan Park? Who did he have in the dark shooting at Ricky? Pretty Boy?

With dark tinted windows so no one could see inside,

Mack drove his car past Big Poppa's crib. Five miles per hour was not the normal speed limit, but he wanted to make sure he did not miss who he was looking for. The block was dead. It seemed unusual. It was Saturday afternoon, one of the busiest days for a hustler. No one was out, so he headed up to the Hole. Mack jumped out of the tinted sedan and walked toward the crowded park. Everybody was out. All eyes were on Mack as he entered the park. He gave everybody a pound as they sat on the wall.

"Yo, Mi, you seen Zeus?"

"Nah he hasn't been around. How's Ricky? I heard he got shot."

"He's alright. You know, one in the leg and one in the stomach. Nothing a doctor couldn't fix though."

~ ~ ~****

As Lo released his jump shot, he noticed Mack coming toward the park. He knew that Mack wasn't coming to chill, but to get information. Lo didn't draw; he continued shooting hoops.

"What's good, lil bro?" Mack said as he greeted Lo.

"Nothing, just shooting around. What happened to Ricky? Heard he caught some hot ones."

"Yeah, he got hit twice, but he should make a full recovery."

"Do you know who did it?" Lo asked, trying to be nosey as Mack smiled.

"Come on, lil bro, that's grown folk's business. What you need to do is keep balling so you can get up out of this mess."

"I'm trying," Lo said as he shot another three hitting nothing but net. "Bro, can you give me a ride to the mall so I can pick up something? Mom gave me forty dollars to buy some shorts, and I want to buy my girl something."

"You got a girl?" Mack asked, but wasn't surprised.

"Come on, Mack. You ain't the only one with girls. Plus, look at these eyes, they're irresistible."

The two brothers laughed as Mack agreed to take his lil brother to the mall. When they got there, it was packed. Mack decided to treat Lo. He ended up walking out of Footlocker with two pairs of sneakers and two pairs of shorts.

"So, what's your girl's name?" Mack asked as they walked through the mall.

"Jazzy. Primo's older sister."

"I know who you're talking about. Diesel's lil cousin."

"Yeah, her, and I fuck with this other chick named Jenny from the lollipop."

"Damn, bro, who do you think you are, me?"

"Nigga, you only got Erica," Lo stated, trying to play his big brother.

"That's what you think."

The brothers joked and laughed together. Lo couldn't remember the last time he had this much fun chilling with Mack. Ever since he had set up shop in the Gardens, they hardly had seen each other. So it really made him feel good that they were bonding right now.

"Who do you like more?"

"I can't decide, bro. They both are good girls, but I think that Jazzy got her."

"Bro, you are too young to be caught up. Just know that you will know who's the one when she pops up in your life and all you can do is think about her and just her. Until then, just play the field and enjoy the ride. So what do you want to buy Jazzy?"

"I was thinking about the heart earrings with her initials inside."

"Aiight, let's get out of here. You won't find that in here."

Mack headed toward Hamilton. It was another spot

that the locals would shop at. They sold clothes, sneakers, jewelry, and all sorts of other shit for the house and anywhere else. Mack pulled up in front of the Indian Boutique.

"When we go in, let me do all the talking," Mack told his lil brother as they entered the store.

"Yo, Mack, long time no see," VJ said, greeting him with a handshake. VJ was the owner of the jewelry part of the store. Anyone looking for a discount price on jewelry, he was the man to see.

"VJ, what's good with you? What do you got for me?"

He laughed. He knew that Mack was a heavy spender. He just put two stacks down on a piece of jewelry the other day that he was buying for himself. It was going to be one of his most prized possessions. "It depends on what you are looking for." He was the type of jeweler that couldn't hold his tongue. He was anxious to expose what the next person just bought. He ran his mouth like the

Boston Marathon. Mack ignored his question.

"I'm here for my little brother. He needs something for his girlfriend. What do you have?" VJ went into his cabinet and showed Lo rings, earrings, and necklaces. He pointed to the rings and necklaces. VJ and Mack went back and forth trying to negotiate a reasonable price for the two. At first Mack felt disrespected about the price he was getting, but they ended up coming up with a good price.

"That's why I fucks with you," Mack said.

"I know," VJ smirked, wrapping the gift up for Lo.

They left the store, and Mack stopped at McDonald's and ordered dinner, when his cellphone rang. Lo saw the look on his face assuming he didn't recognize the number, but he answered it anyway.

"Who's this? Sorry, ma, I'm eating."

"Business?" Lo asked.

"Nah, Ricky left his house. He's walking around with

a cane, when he's supposed to be at home resting. You trying to go for this ride?"

"Yes," Lo replied as he munched on his fries. "Plus, I haven't seen Ricky since that day you had all that money in the room."

"You remember that?" Mack said.

"How can I forget. What was it, a million dollars?"

Mack laughed. "Nah, bro, only twenty thousand."

"Shit, that's still a lot of money, especially to me."

"Listen, bro, it's not about how much money you got, it's all about what you do with it. You can have it today and it can disappear tomorrow. Remember that, bro, because that's one of the most important lessons you will ever learn in life. Make sure that you make the money, and not let the money make you."

"So what are you going to do with your money?"

"You sound like ma with all the cop questions."

"I just want to know."

"Aiight. Invest your money into something that you're good at or love doing. If you got five dollars, figure out a way to turn that five into ten, ten to a hundred. But try not to go backward, and never tell anyone your plans or how much you have."

"Okay!"

"Be a boss and leader. Let people follow your lead, and always help those that are in need. Never burn your bridges, because once you do, you'll lose them forever. You never know when you might need to walk over that bridge."

Lo loved to get schooled by his brother. Mack didn't realize that Lo was soaking up all the knowledge so he could run his own crew soon. He knew that Mack was venting and exposing how he was running the Gardens, so he was all ears. After circling around the Center City blocks searching for Ricky, they found him out front of

Rico's barbershop.

"What the fuck you doing here? Mom is worried about you, and sent me out looking for you," Mack yelled out the driver's-side window. "Get in the fucking car."

Mack could see the pain in Ricky's eyes as he hobbled to the car. Ricky noticed Lo in the passenger seat and hopped in the back.

"You ain't answer my question," Mack yelled. "You know who shop that is?"

"It's just a barbershop," Lo said, confused. "But whose?"

"Do you know whose shop that is?" Ricky said sarcastically.

"Yeah, Rico's! Fuck you doing there?"

Once Mack said the name, it popped into Lo's head. Rico. He remembered the night in Mack's room when they had money all over the bed. Mack mentioned Rico's name. The dude that they had robbed was one of his men.

Lo was putting two and two together.

"I think I saw one of Rico's cars the day I got shot."

"You're delusional. I told you to give it some time. I'm sure you know who's behind all this, but you need to focus on getting better."

Ricky stood quiet as Mack scolded him the entire ride home. Mack spun a few blocks and double-parked in front of Ricky's house. They dapped each other up, and Mack watched Ricky enter his house. Mack then dropped Lo off.

~ ~ ~

After two weeks of recovery, Ricky was finally on his feet walking without the cane. He was like a one-year-old who finally learned how to walk. He was all over the place.

"Ricky," Isabel yelled from the first floor. "Mack's outside beeping."

"I'll be right out," he yelled out the window, hoping that

Mack could hear him. Ricky ran down the stairs and headed toward the door.

"Wait, Ricky," Isabel shouted as she grabbed her son by the arm.

He turned around to face his mother, who was in tears. "What's wrong, Mom?"

"I had a horrible dream, hijo. You need to be real careful out there," she said as she wiped the tears from her eyes. "In my dream, I saw you running through an alley bleeding from head to toe." She placed her head on his chest.

"Everything is going to be okay, ma, don't worry." He kissed her on top of her head. "I love you!"

"I love you too, Ricardo," she said back.

Ricky was stunned. He knew that she was serious. Isabel hasn't mentioned his real name since his father left ten years ago. She had a similar dream, but that time was about his father. She dreamed that Ricardo Sr. had picked up and left her. He pleaded that he would never leave her and their family. Then one morning he left work after his normal day, and never returned home. She was still haunted by her dreams to this day. The sun's ray blinded Ricky as he walked outside. He was shocked to see Mack stunting in his new ride.

"What's this? You making moves without me?" Ricky said, analyzing the whip.

"Nah, bro, just grabbed this off Lou's Garage. Something light, hop in." Ricky hopped in the passenger seat with ease. "So how's the body? Healed up?"

"Doctor said that everything looks good and I'm cleared to hit the field." They both laughed.

"Heard from Zeus?" Mack asked.

"Nah. I tried calling and paging him, and I got nothing."

"I've been looking around for him myself. And his team has been MIA. I don't trust Zeus. I ran your story over and over in my head trying to get around it. I think he set you up to get murdered." Ricky didn't respond. He thought differently.

"What we doing up here?" Ricky asked as they pulled into the Hole.

"I gotta see Diesel. Since you've been playing commando with Zeus, I've been making moves with him. I put the Gardens on my back. Next, I want the town, then the state. I got a vision, Ricky, and a plan. I refuse to let anyone hold me back."

Ricky felt like those last eight words were meant for him. "When was you going to run shit by me?" he asked.

"I tried to put you on after we robbed Rico, but you was too busy looking fresh and buying jewelry and shit. You didn't seem interested, so I made my own move."

"Yeah, I feel you." Ricky said in a low tone. He felt betrayed. The whole time he thought Mack was still running for Big T, and all along he was making power moves. "I feel you," he said again, this time it was sarcastically.

The moment was awkward. Neither of them spoke as Mack pulled up and parked on Bradford Street, outside of Diesel's mother's house.

FOURTEEN

"JUNITO, JUICE, Y'ALL READY?"

"Come on, cuz, we deep in this shit."

Junito stood quietly as he stared at his chrome .357 snub nose. He raised his gun to his lips, kissed it, and said. "I'm ready!" Mack knew that Junito was a gat, but now was the time to see what he really was made of.

"The white house on the left," Mack said as he drove by. He circled the block again, then parked the car in front of the house.

"Junito and I are going in. Juice, you take the wheel. If we ain't out in ten minutes, you come in blazing."

"I got you," Juice replied.

Junito and Mack exited the SUV and headed toward the white house. "Don't look like anyone's home."

"Nobody's supposed to be here. This is the stash

house. We gonna get all this work, and if anyone is home, you know what to do."

As they entered the house, there wasn't a soul in sight. The solid oak floors came to life as they inched across the kitchen.

"Check the closets and the basement. I'm going to check the bedrooms out. We're looking for some bricks, and a duffle bag of weed," Mack said.

He tippy-toed up the wooden steps, gun drawn. The way he maneuvered in and out of the rooms with his gun aimed at the ready, he looked like he had taken classes at the police academy. Each room was empty.

"Fuck, I hope Junito has better luck."

"Fuck, this shit is empty," Junito mumbled as he searched the living room closet.

He had no patience. Instead of opening the basement door slowly, he yanked it open almost taking it off the hinges. He flicked on the basement lights and walked down the old wooden steps. He was hit instantly by the aroma of weed. He realized that he had hit the jackpot. On the ground sat two duffle bags and two separate book bags. He opened the two duffle bags and saw pounds of weed bagged up.

He zipped them back up and crouched over the book bags, unzipping the first one and finding two bricks of crack. They were neatly wrapped and untouched. He lifted the other one; it was also heavy. He unzipped it, and to his surprise, there were six guns and two suppressors. He zipped both book bags back up and placed the bags across his wide shoulders, then headed upstairs. When he got to the top of the steps, Mack was waiting for him.

"You got it?"

"Yup. Grab these two book bags. I got the bud."

They quickly exited the house, hopped in the SUV and headed toward Mack's house. The drive was long and quiet. The aroma of bud filled the air. The trio was in riding mode and was focused on the plan. They dropped off the bud, coke, and guns and drove to an apartment complex off of Tillman Street. A gate stopped all traffic from entering. The premises were fully secured. Unless you were a resident, you couldn't enter. Juice, Junito, and Mack waited patiently for someone to enter or exit so they could make their move inside the apartment complex and not abort the mission.

"Let's get out of here. We got the first house. That should put a dent in Zeus's pockets."

~ ~ ~

Lo's dream got interrupted as he heard the front door slam. Ever since he started hustling, he had been paranoid. He looked at his alarm clock and it read 1:21 a.m. He hopped out of bed and headed toward Mack's room. There was a strong odor seeping through the cracks of Mack's door. Lo was nosey, so he opened the door slowly.

The smell of weed hit his nostrils. He clicked on the bedroom light and noticed two duffle bags sat in the center of the floor. He quickly turned off the light and ran downstairs. The living room was empty. He checked the locks on the door, then headed back to Mack's room. He clicked on the lights again and left the door slightly ajar.

Lo unzipped one duffle bag, and his eyes lit up. There were bags and bags of green weed. He had never seen that much weed in his young life. On Mack's bed sat two book bags. He opened the first one and saw six guns. He quickly closed it. He opened the second one. Inside were two neatly square blocks, wrapped in black tape. Lo had no idea what it was, so he zipped it back up and went back to the bud.

He grabbed one of the pounds and opened it. The smell of fresh weed got him excited. He went to Mack's paraphernalia drawer and grabbed a handful of weed and placed it in the first sandwich bag. He filled it to its capacity. He continued the same process with three other pound bags and filled the rest of the sandwich bags.

All of a sudden, he heard his front screen door come to life. He knew that his brother was home. He quickly sealed the blemished pounds of weed, zipped the duffle bag, turned off the light, closed the door and ran to the bathroom.

He heard voices coming up the stairs. He recognized Mack's and Juice's voice. He went to the hamper, grabbed a dirty shirt and wrapped the weed in it. He crept out of the bathroom like a church mouse. He lay in his bed fully awake, contemplating all the money that he was going make.

~ ~ ~

"Damn, these joints ain't even been touched yet. We gonna make a killing off this," Juice said.

"We gotta cut Diesel a piece off of the two bricks. The bud is all ours," Mack said.

"What's his cut?"

"Thirty thousand. Fifteen a brick."

Junito got angry. "Diesel don't deserve shit. We did all the work."

"If it wasn't for Diesel, we wouldn't have shit. What's fifteen per brick, when we got 'bout fifty pounds for ourselves?" Junito agreed and nodded his head. "So, Junito, what do you want? Coke or weed?" Mack asked.

"Neither, I just want to blow a nigga's face off," he said, holding up his gun.

"Slow down, homie. There will be a time for that." Mack smiled. "Right now, we gotta get this money. So this is what we are going to do. Tomorrow we head up to Indian Boutique and buy the biggest dime bags they have. We gonna flood the hood with the fattest sacks. With the coke, we gonna cook it up, get it to all the young boys and flood the blocks. That way the Gardens will be known for crack and bud."

"What 'bout Fat Freddy?" Juice asked. "They been

selling weed up there for years."

"I'ma holla at him. We won't interrupt his flow on Dauphin. We gonna stay on the strip," Mack replied.

"And if he act a fool, we run him out," Junito said as he analyzed the guns with suppressors.

"Exactly, but we'll give him a chance to get down first."

~ ~ ~

The following morning, they headed to Indian Boutique as planned. VJ got them the biggest jewelry bags that they had.

"Damn, how many dimes is that?" Juice asked, looking at his fingertips.

"I don't know, but my tips are aching," Mack said.

"These shits don't even close."

"Half of them are still open. So we gonna have to burn the tips to make them shut." They all looked in the direction of the door when it opened.

"Mack, what you doing? The house smells like weed," Lo said as he walked in. His eyes widened. "Mom is going to kill you when she comes home."

"Chill, Lo, we good," said Mack.

"What's up, Juice?" Lo said as he looked at the unfamiliar face that was there also.

"What's up, lil cuz?" Juice said as he grabbed Lo in a chokehold. Lo tapped out instantly.

"Who's the new face?"

"Bro, that's Junito. He's new on the team. Junito, that's my little brother Lo."

"If that's your lil brother, then that's my lil brother too," he said as he went to dap Lo.

~ ~ ~

It'd been almost four weeks since Ricky had been on the block. Recovering from his gunshot wounds and getting high, his money was starting to decline. He'd been hitting Zeus's cell phone up, but he has been avoiding him. He was down to his last two stacks. Ricky grabbed his gun out of his drawer and thought about doing a lick. He walked out of the crib with robbery on his mind.

As he turned the corner on Nineth Street, from a distance he could see a crowd outside Rico's barbershop. He was looking for trouble, and that was a hustler's worst nightmare. When a killer's stomach is touching, there's no picks; everyone is a target.

As cocky and arrogant as Ricky was, he strolled down Ninth Street, same side as the barbershop. He noticed Rico's Range Rover. Before he drew any attention, he crossed the street unnoticed. He sat on Big Poppa's vacant porch and staked out the busy shop. He took a glance at his iced-out Aqua Master watch: 7:55. He should be closing up soon, he thought. After hours of contemplating, Ricky paced back and forth, then went past the shop and posted up. Rico's driver exited the shop and jumped into the Range.

The engine roared. Through the driver's-side mirror, Ricky noticed that the driver was busy on the phone. He made his move. He slipped into the shop gun drawn. He knew if Rico was on point, this could cost him his life, but he didn't care. His life was already fucked up ever since Pretty Boy introduced him to Juice joints. Rico's back was toward Ricky. He put the barrel of his weapon to his head.

"Caught you slipping. Run that shit, nigga!"

"You gonna rob me in my own spot?"

Ricky slapped him in the back of his head with the butt of the gun. Blood started oozing out. "Run that shit."

Rico tried to turn to see the robber's face. Ricky reacted quickly and split his forehead with the gun. The ski mask disguised his identity anyway. Rico fell to the ground in pain.

"I'm a kill you," Rico said. "You got this. Here!" He went in his pocket and pulled out a knot full of hundred-dollar bills and passed it to Ricky.

"Where the safe at?" Ricky demanded as he grabbed the stack. "I know there's more."

At this point Ricky was sweating. He knew that at any moment the driver could come back in and a shoot-out could occur. Before he could make another move, Rico crawled to his desk and pulled out a small safe.

"Here! Now get the fuck out of here."

Ricky grabbed the safe and ran toward the exit. A cool breeze hit Ricky as he stepped out of the barbershop. He looked back over his shoulder to see if Rico was following him. The coast was clear. To avoid any suspicions or police interactions, he slid off the ski mask. He got away, robbing the boss clean.

~ ~ ~

"Oh shit, Crystal, look. Someone wearing a ski mask just came out of Rico's barbershop."

"Babe, he's coming our way. Close the blinds."

"Honey, he's not paying us any attention. I think he just robbed Rico."

"Do you think he killed him?"

"I didn't hear any shots."

"Babe, look. He took off his ski mask. Do you know who he is?"

"Oh shit. He's one of those guys that be chilling with Big Poppa. I think his name is Ricky."

"Yup, that's him. Do you think he robbed him?"

"I don't know. All I know is if he robbed Rico and Rico finds out, Ricky is a dead man."

"Babe, do you think you can negotiate this information with one of Rico's workers so we can get a hit? I need to get high."

"You fucking right. I'm a call Sonny right now."

FIFTEEN

BOOM! BOOM! BOOM!

Lo knocked on the front door. A voice came from inside of AR's house.

"Who is it?"

"Lo, is AR home?"

"Yeah, come in. He's in his room," AR's mom said.

Lo ran up the stairs anxiously to see his friend. Without even knocking Lo opened the door. "Yo, I got some shit for you."

"Damn, can I at least get some dap?" AR asked.

"No doubt," Lo replied as he gave him a pound. "Look what I got for you." Before Lo could pull out what he had, AR pulled out a .22 long nose. Lo jumped back. "Where the hell you get that from?"

"The neighbor next door gave it to me. He wanted me to hold it down, so I told him I would. I'ma rob me a muthafucka with this bitch."

"Man, you ain't gotta rob anyone. That's why I came to see your crazy ass. Look what I got for you." Lo pulled out a sandwich bag full of weed and held it up in the air for AR to see. His eyes lit up at the sight of the bag Lo was holding.

"Where did you get that from?"

Lo couldn't tell him that he just robbed Mack, so he lied. "I got it from Rock. Come on, let's bag all of this shit up in nicks. I'll let you push it so you can make some money."

"Good look, Lo. You're a real fucking lifesaver. I was about to go out there and do something stupid. I was going to catch me a nigga sleeping and jam his dumb ass," AR said as he gripped the revolver.

"Put that shit away. We don't need that shit unless

someone tries to rob one of us. For now, let's focus on this money."

AR went to the kitchen to grab some sandwich bags out of the drawer. He rushed back up to his room so they could get to work on the weed. After an hour of bagging up, they counted eighty nickel bags. AR took twenty bags as the pair headed to the park.

"Don't forget, we split the profit down the middle when you're done."

~ ~ ~

"Where you at?" Erica yelled through the phone.

"I'm in the hood, why?"

"Because I haven't heard from you in a week. Did you forget that you had a girl?"

"No, I didn't forget that I have a girlfriend. Besides, you're not just my girl, you're wifey. I've just been busy." Mack's phone went dead.

"I thought you didn't have a girl, or should I say wifey?" Lori asked.

On the low, Mack had been scooping her up any chance he got. They would mostly meet up on late nights when she could sneak out and chill with him. He could keep it one hundred with her, and she kept her mouth closed because she wanted to see him again.

"That is my ex. I have to treat her like she's still my girl until I get all my stuff from her crib. The bitch is crazy and will destroy all my personal stuff if I don't. Now, where were we? So your mom doesn't like dope boy's gun?" he said quickly, changing the subject.

"No, she can't stand you. She thinks that all y'all need to get a real job and not stand on the street poisoning our friends, loved ones, etc. She also hates when y'all be making all that noise in the middle of the night."

Mack laughed at Lori's comment as they sat in his tinted car. "Well I'll tell the fellas to keep it down."

Lori looked at him. "You don't have pull like that. Who do you think you are, the boss or something?"

"You must not know me like that."

Lori ignored him. "You know I love your smile, Mack." As she leaned in and kissed him, she immediately placed her hand on his jewels. His manhood twitched. He could feel his erection trying to make way through his clothes. Lori began sucking on his lips and moaning at the same time. Mack knew that he was about to fuck her.

He grabbed Lori out of her seat and placed her on his lap. She started to grind on his dick, whispering in his ear. "I'm so wet, papi. Here's an early birthday present." She had a devilish grin on her face.

Fog started to fill the car windows as they breathed heavily in excitement. She unbuttoned her Daisy Dukes and removed Mack's hand from her ass. With her tongue still in his mouth, she scooted up her hips to remove her shorts, revealing her laced pink thong.

The mood was heating up. Mack slid his sweatpants down, releasing his erection. He thought about stopping because he didn't have a condom, but Lori insisted. She grabbed his dick and filled her sex. Lori gave off a loud moan. He could feel her juices as she rocked back and forth, up and down on his shaft. Mack leaned the driver's seat all the way back so Lori could get the full ride.

"I can feel it in my stomach," she whispered in his ear. That turned him on even more. He clutched on her ass and she grinded harder and faster as the tip of his dick was rubbing against her stomach.

"Wait, wait," Mack yelled, but it was too late. The both of them came simultaneously. She kissed Mack's neck as he laid his kids all up inside her.

"Maybe next time we can be in a more comfortable spot."

"Maybe," Lori said as she eased off his dick and sat in the passenger seat. She then cleaned herself off. "Thank you!" she said as she gave him a sweet kiss goodbye.

SIXTEEN

MACK PULLED UP TO RICKY'S CRIB AS HIS CELL

phone rang.

"Yo, Mack, where you at?" Juice asked.

"What's up with the loud music in the background? I'm
on my way to pick up Ricky."

"Come to Jessica's crib. She's having a get-together."

"Word. Who all up there? You know it's my birthday
in a couple of hours," Mack said.

"Yeah, we know, so let's celebrate early. Everyone is
up here. Jessica even invited her friends from the city."

"Say no more. I'ma grab Ricky real quick then swing
over there so I can introduce him to the family."

"Okay, cuz. You know where to find me at." They
ended their call, and then he pulled up at Ricky's crib. He

got out and walked up to the door, tapping it lightly. Isabel answered right away.

"Hello Isabel, is Ricky home?"

"Yes, baby, come in. He's in his room."

"Okay, ma, I'll go up and get him.

"Wait, wait, Mack. I need to talk to you."

"What happened, ma. Is everything okay?"

Isabel pulled out a stem. She told him all about Ricky's late nights out with Pretty Boy. She said she felt like he was on stronger drugs than weed. From the look of the stem, Mack knew he probably was smoking crack, but he didn't say anything to Isabel because he didn't want to worry her. He grabbed the stem from her and headed up to Ricky's room. He barged in without knocking, but Ricky was nowhere in sight.

"Ricky!" Mack yelled. "Ricky!" All you could hear was the AC running. In a quick second Mack heard a mouse noise coming from the closet. He walked directly to the door and swung it open. In the closet, Mack saw a familiar sight that fucked him up, a sight that he had seen plenty of times from the fiends in the Hole. Ricky was curled up in the fetal position, shaking. Mack yanked him out of the closet.

"What the fuck is you doing? I know you're not high on crack. What the fuck is wrong with you, nigga?" Mack yelled at him.

Ricky's jaw was stuck. He tried to force words out of his mouth. "I'm, I'm sssooorrryyy!"

Mack grabbed him by his sweaty shirt and pulled him up to his feet like he was a ragdoll. "Who the fuck introduced you to this shit?"

"I, I, was sma, sma, smoking with Z, Z, Zeus and Pe, Le, Prett, t, ty Boy. I think they laced the weed."

Mack gave Ricky a tight hug. "It's okay, bro. I got you. I'ma take care of you. Come on and jump in the shower, so we can clean you up. We have a party to go to."

Ricky pointed toward the bed. "That bag is for you. Happy birthday, bro."

Even through all the drugs Ricky still had the courtesy to get him a birthday gift. As Ricky took a shower, Mack looked inside of the bag to see what he had gotten him. Inside was two Polo shirts and two pairs of Levi jeans. Once Ricky was done showering and getting dressed, they were ready to roll.

The two killers looked stunning as they left the house. Mack wore his fresh white-and-blue sevens that hadn't even hit the stores yet, blue Polo jeans and a white Polo shirt that had a navy-blue horse, and a navy-blue Yankee fitted that sat low, covering his eyes.

Ricky slipped on his all-black LRG pants, black-and-gold Air Forces, black LRG shirt with the gold print, and black-and-gold Pittsburgh Pirates cap, with his big Cuban link chain.

"Those bitches are going to be on our dicks when we get there," Mack stated.

"I know."

Through their excitement, conversing about their get-together they were about to attend, they failed to check their surroundings. Rico and three of his gunmen watched as Mack and Ricky got in the car. Word got out that Ricky was responsible for robbing the boss, and he wanted revenge.

As Mack pulled out of the parking space, Ricky started to tell that he needed to fill him in on what he had done a few days ago.

"Mack, I fucked up."

"It's okay, bro, we gonna take care of you."

"I'm not talking about that."

Mack was confused. He looked at Ricky with a strange look on his face. "What you talking about?"

"The other day I was hit. I needed money. I tried calling Zeus to get some work, but he never answered, and I was afraid to call you."

"All you gotta do is ask. You know I got you," Mack interrupted.

"I know, but I didn't want to tell you that I fucked up all the money. So I took into my own hands."

Mack looked at Ricky again as he drove down Seventh Street. "What did you do?"

"I waited until all the barbers left the barbershop, and I ran up on Rico and robbed him."

"YOU DID WHAT?" Mack yelled.

"I robbed him, and I pistol-whipped his ass too."

Mack started punching the steering wheel in anger. "What the fuck is wrong with you? You know if he finds out, he's going to try and kill you."

"I ain't scared of that nigga," Ricky yelled back at

Mack. "Fuck Rico. I put in my own work. Is you riding or what?"

Mack ignored his question, trying to piece things together in his mind. Mack went instantly into war mode. He started focusing on the cars behind him. He had the art of war down to a science. Wars are like a game of chess, and each move is considered costly.

"Is you riding or what?" Ricky asked again.

Mack glanced at Ricky before he spoke, looking directly into his eyes.

"You know I'm riding. Just next time you're in a position like that, holla at me first. From now on you're not leaving my sight. You got a twenty-four-hour duty in the Gardens. You'll be safe and comfortable up there."

From a distance, Mack noticed a car speeding, trying to catch up to them. He smoothly swerved past two cars to see if the speeding car was tailing them.

"Ricky, get ready. I think we got a tail." He pulled out

his chrome Desert Eagle, placed it on his lap, and looked through the visor mirror. "I'ma make this left on Turner. Jump out. If this black SUV turns right after me, let them have it."

Mack quickly made the left turn and parked up in front of an old church. The moment Ricky jumped out the passenger side, the black SUV made a sharp turn, tires screeching. Ricky didn't hesitate. He fired instantly.

POP! POP! POP! POP!

Bullets banged off the metal frame.

POP! POP! POP! POP!

The driver window shattered. The SUV started swerving recklessly, passing Ricky. He let off four more rounds, emptying the clip. The occupants in the SUV had no chance to fire back. Mack and Ricky were always ready for war, always on point and two steps ahead. What they didn't know was that they were dealing with a different type of enemy, enemies that have been in all types of war.

Rico was just as intelligent, if not more intelligent, than Mack and Ricky. Before Rico started a war, he liked to see who he was dealing with. So he liked to test the waters a bit. While Mack and Ricky were arguing about what Ricky had done, Rico noticed that the driver of the car kept glancing in his rearview mirror an odd number of times. From that moment, Rico knew that the driver was on point. He pulled out his AK and pointed it at a man in a black SUV. As the man swerved in and out of lanes, Rico followed him as if he was chasing him.

Rico noticed the change in speed from Mack's car, noticing that they made a detour on Turner Street, and what a coincidence, the SUV made the same left, following them. As Rico's driver stopped the pursuit and kept driving up Seventh Street, they heard the shots. Rico knew that Ricky and the unknown driver were on point and was quick to pull the trigger at any moment.

"They are going to be a fucking problem," Rico said,

leaning back in his seat.

SEVENTEEN

WHEN MACK ENTERED JESSICA'S, THE WHOLE

house erupted with all kinds of "HAPPY BIRTHDAYS!"

Mack froze in shock. He had never been surprised, let

alone caught off guard. He was always two steps ahead

of everyone, but not this time. He had been so caught up

into Ricky's mayhem, he didn't even assume that the get-

together was for him. Juice was the first one to greet him.

"Happy birthday, cuz. Was you surprised?"

"You fucking right, I was. You got me good. Whose

idea was this?"

"All of ours."

Mack gave Juice a tight hug. "Good looking, cuz.

Juice, this is my right-hand man, Ricky. Ricky, this is my

heart, Juice."

"I heard all about you," Juice said.

"Same here," said Ricky.

"Juice, get the team together. I want to introduce everyone to Ricky. We gonna be in Rob's room," Mack said.

Before Mack could even make it up the steps, he ran into his little brother.

"Happy birthday, bro."

"Thanks, bro. What brings you up here?"

"You know I couldn't miss your birthday party. Besides, the Garden got them hoes out."

Mack laughed. "I better not catch you smoking or drinking. But, look, I gotta holla at the fellas real quick. I'll get up with you in a few."

Lo looked at his brother, who was always about business. This was his birthday, and he wanted to bust it up with the fellas about business.

"Aiight, bro, say no more," Lo said as he gave him and

Ricky some dap.

Mack introduced Ricky to the team one by one. He assigned him to the top lot, Juice to the center and the mailboxes, and Husky and Vic to the bottom. He said if money came in loads, stash it with Rob.

"And what does he do?" Ricky asked, pointing to Junito.

"Don't worry about what I do. Worry about yourself ," Junito chimed in, a lil agitated.

"Nigga, you don't know me," Ricky stated with his hand gripping his empty gun.

"Junito is my muscle. He ain't chasing paper," Mack said, looking into Ricky's eyes.

"Nah, I ain't into that, partna," Junito said as he pulled out his baby, his .357 snub nose. "This is what I'm into right here."

Ricky saw it coming. He instantly pulled out his Desert

Eagle and held it to his side.

"And who says I ain't?"

"Fellas, fellas. Put y'all's shit away," Mack ordered.

"We are on the same fucking team. We should be worried about getting this fucking money and the niggas that might want to try and take it away. There's no need to beef with one another." Junito eyed Ricky as he placed his gun back on his hip. Mack looked at Ricky. "And since we on the gun convo, we gonna need some more firearms."

"I'll holla at my peoples in the city," Vic said.

Mack could still sense the tension between Junito and Ricky. He knew that there would be a problem between the two of them in the near future.

"Juice, stay put. I need to speak with you for a minute," Mack said as everyone was exiting the room.

"What's up, birthday boy? Everything good?"

"Look, cuz. We just got into a shootout on the way up

here."

"Shoot out! With who?" Juice asked, interrupting Mack.

"I don't think it was for me. I think it was for Ricky, but we was on point. Ricky aired them out. All I know is that he got into some shit with this kingpin from Center City named Rico. He robbed him, and if he found out that it was Ricky, I'm sure that there's a price on his head."

Juice listened and wasn't happy with what he had just heard.

"Look, cuz, that's going to bring too much heat to the hood. We just put this plan into motion, and already your man got us on high alert. He's already beefing with Junito. He's got to go."

"Ricky's not going anywhere, cuz. He's safe up here, as long as word doesn't get back to Rico."

"If your man gets shit hot, cuz, I'ma take him out myself," Juice said, clutching his Glock .40.

"If he gets out of line and jeopardizes my family, I'll do it myself. F.O.E. for life," Mack said.

"Family Over Everything," Juice said.

"But let's not jump the gun. Just keep an eye on him for me."

Juice looked at Mack, mad. "Man, I ain't babysitting no one, cuz."

"Just keep him tamed."

"Say no more. Now let's party."

Jessica grabbed Mack as he entered the room and yelled, "Happy birthday!" over the music.

"Did you see my homegirl that I brought down from New York?" Jessica walked Mack over to where her friend was standing. "Princess, this is my cousin Mack that I was telling you about."

Mack looked at her like she was one of the finest women he'd seen in a while.

"Hello, Princess, how . . ." Before he could finish, she spoke up.

"Happy birthday. Let's take a shot," she said, pulling Mack into the kitchen. Mack was paying extra attention to her body. She was a flawless dime piece. "What would you like to drink, Henny, Bacardi?"

"I'll take Bacardi, since it's soft. I don't want you burning your chest with that Hen-Rock."

"Oh, you trying to be sweet, or what, you spitting game?" Princess laughed as she poured two shots of Bacardi.

"Nah, ma, I haven't started to spit game yet."

"So, when are you going to start?" she thought to herself, then let out a soft giggle. She passed him a shot and made a toast. "To Mack. Happy birthday, and I pray that you have many more." She tapped his glass. "Your turn!"

"I want to make a toast for a grateful future and a

separate toast to my beautiful girl Princess," he said, tapping glasses with her again quickly before she caught what he said, and they threw them back.

"That was smooth, Mack, but who said I wanted to be your girl?" she replied, letting him know that she heard what he said. Mack looked her up and down.

"Why wouldn't you want to?" They both laughed.

"You're crazy, boy. Go enjoy your party." As she walked off, she looked back and said, "Don't forget to save a dance for me." Then walked into the living room.

Mack exited the party and hit the strip, where all the guys were sitting around hanging out. He scooted down and fixed his pants.

"What do we have going on over here? The party is over there. I see we are all getting along," he said, sending subliminal messages to Ricky and Junito.

"Yeah, we good," Junito said. "Just showing the brother the hood and his post."

"What about me, Mack? Where's my spot," Lo asked.

Mack laughed. "Your spot is at school, in them books."

"Give the lil nigga a pack. He gotta learn the family business one day," Ricky said.

Mack got furious. He got directly in Ricky's face. "My lil brother ain't getting involved in this life, and if I catch any of you passing him a pack, I'll personally blow your fucking face off all over this fucking ground. You got that? Don't disrespect me again."

"Chill, Mack, I was just joking," Ricky said, holding up his hands in a surrendering position.

"I don't joke like that when it comes to my lil brother. I want a better life for him. That's why I do what I do. Let me get back to the party before I lose my cool. Lo, let me know if you need a ride home. And don't pay no mind to these assholes."

The DJ had slowed the party down as Mack walked

through the door. H.E.R was blasting through the speakers. Mack saw Princess slow dancing with Jessica. He grabbed her by the waist and pulled her away from his cousin. She was surprised.

He whispered in her ear, "You ready for this dance? It's a perfect song."

Princess didn't say a word. Her actions spoke for her. She grabbed Mack's hand that was sitting on her waist and started moving her body side to side. Mack turned Princess around so that they were face to face. She wrapped her arms around his neck, staring into his eyes. She noticed that his eyes were dark, like he had no soul.

"You have beautiful eyes," he said.

"Thank you!"

"You're also very beautiful."

"You ain't too bad yourself," Princess said, and they both laughed together, interrupting their motion.

"I don't think you can handle a woman like me. You're still a young boy."

"Damn, that's how you feel? You're trying to play me now."

"Nah, I'm playing with you, but do you think you're ready for me?"

"You think you're ready for a G like me?" He was seriously attracted to her, but he had to play it cool.

Princess looked into his eyes, this time with a cold stare. "I don't want a G Mack. I want a man." She smiled, and before he could respond, she leaned forward and kissed him. They were so caught up in the moment that neither of them realized that they were the only ones left on the dance floor. Cell phone cameras started flashing as they kissed. The entire room erupted. Jessica hugged them both as she interrupted their kiss.

"You better take care of her, Mack."

"She's in good hands," Mack replied.

The DJ switched the vibe and turned the party into a frenzy. Meek Millz filled the room. Princess pulled Mack out of the crowded living room, headed to the kitchen and out back.

"So let me know a little about you, Mack."

"What do you want to know?"

"I want to know who Mack is, and what your plans for the future are."

Mack was caught off guard with her question. "I'ma be honest with you, ma. My plan is to get my family out of the struggle. I grew up without a dad. My step pops raised me since I was a baby. All I've seen was my father's hustle. Once he got locked up, my mother suffered and struggled ever since. So I have to get my family straight by any means."

"And how are you gonna do that?" Princess asked.

"The only way I know ma, hustling."

"So, you're a dope boy?"

"You can say that, but I'm past the hand to hands, or standing on the block shit. I run this hood."

"And what do you plan on doing with the money you're making?"

He was getting a little uncomfortable with her questions, so he flipped it on her.

"Enough about me, ma, what you about?"

"Well I'm a senior in high school, and I'm graduating next week. I plan on going to NYU. I want to get my master's degree in business and attend pediatric classes. I love kids. I take care of my little brother, Christopher, who is eleven, and my little sister, Diamond. She's six. Do you have any brothers and sisters?"

"Yeah. My older brother Husky and my little brother Lo. They both are here. And I have a little sister, Marie. I see you got a good head on your shoulders. I like that."

"I told you, Mack, are you sure that you're ready for a lady like me?" Princess asked again.

"I'm ready, ma, I promise," Mack replied as he leaned in and kissed her soft lips.

He felt like it was love at first sight. He knew that Princess was the one. He instantly got that tingle in his gut the moment they met. Every time she spoke or touched him, the tingling sensation was still present. They both chilled outside of Jessica's house talking 'bout their families and their future goals the entire night.

EIGHTEEN

(ONE WEEK LATER)

After hanging in the Gardens at Mack's birthday party, Lo decided that the Gardens was going to be his temporary stomping grounds. He felt the love when he was around his family and Mack's crew. They were all close, and considered each other as family, not friends. It was a totally different atmosphere than the Hole. Even though Lo was loyal to his friends and the Hole, he felt like everyone was out for themselves. No unity. It was like everyone was competing with each other, instead of being a team.

In the Gardens everyone ate. They each took turns making sales. That was the way Mack ran things. They were organized. So Lo wanted to get more information and watch how Mack organized his team so he could do the same thing in the Hole, but with his team.

Juice greeted Lo with open arms when he saw him.

"What's up, cuz?"

"Nothing really. Just seeing what's up here. Where's Mack?"

"He just went to M&A's to grab some Dutches. You trying to smoke?" Juice said while inhaling the marijuana smoke.

"You heard Mack flipped out on Ricky at his party. He wouldn't like that."

"You good with me, cuzzo. I ain't saying shit," Juice said while passing Lo the Dutch.

Lo took a big hit of the weed, trying to impress Juice. A cloud of smoke filled his little lungs. His chest burned. As much as he tried to hold the smoke in, he choked and started coughing up his lungs.

"What the fuck is that?" Lo slurred.

Juice busted out laughing as Lo bent over coughing,

then dropped to his knees. He placed his hands on the floor gasping for air.

"That's that gungy right there. No one told you to try to hit it like a big man. This isn't no regular shit that they sell in the Hole. Now get your ass up before Mack comes back."

"You could have warned me," Lo said, trying to breathe.

After he was able to get his wind back, Juice tried to pass him the weed again, but he declined the offer. He was already feeling the effect of the potency. In the distance Lo heard thumping. Sounds of loud music coming from an automobile's subwoofers. The song was familiar to Lo, it was a single from Da Baby, one of Mack's favorite songs. He drove slowly through his hood looking at everybody that was on the strip.

"Where the girls at?" Lo asked his cousin.

"They're all over. You just gotta find them."

Lo was so high that he went into a trance and started daydreaming about the time they played the Garden in flag football. There were at least twenty girls cheering for the home team and booing the away team as they arrived. All the boos didn't affect their game though. Lo threw eight touchdown passes, and thanks to his fat cousin Macho, he ran two kick returns back for touchdowns. He cracked a smile as he thought about the pretty faces in the crowd.

"I hope I run into them," Lo thought to himself.

Mack was approaching. "What's up, lil bro? What you doing up here?"

"Just checking the scene out. Seeing where I'ma post up at." Mack giggled, not paying any attention to Lo's comments. Then his smile turned into a serious look. Before Mack could respond, Lo redeemed himself. "Nah, I'm playing, bro. Just tired of the Hole. I need a change of scenery."

"Okay. Just be careful. If you need anything, let me or

Juice know."

What Mack didn't know was that Lo was up there observing and taking notes. He wanted to get a full picture of how Mack ran things. While up there, he noticed that Mack didn't do hand to hand sales in the Gardens. He only made sales to his personal fiends that texted him.

Through conversations he learned that Mack only cooked up his product and distributed it to Juice. He only spoke to Juice about his drug business and how it was moving.

Lo wanted to be in the same position as his brother, but he knew there was still a lot to learn, and he had to be patient and wait his turn.

~ ~ ~

"AR, what's good? How we looking?" Lo asked.

"Nigga, I been done with that. Where you been? I've been looking for you for days."

"My bad, I got stuck on the south side with my brother.

He got that shit on lock, plus I was chilling with Missy."

"Angel's shorty?"

"Yup!"

"Damn. Shit, who else you ran into up there?"

"All the females from the gym. They all talked shit to me when they saw me."

"I need an invite next time," AR said. "Look, I got that money for the weed. You got more?"

"I gotta holla at Rock, plus I gotta re-up. I'll let you know when I'm ready."

"Bet. Did you hear the news?"

"Nah, what happened?"

"Word floating around that someone robbed Zeus for the mother lode. Two bricks and a hundred pounds of weed a couple of weeks ago. Zeus been questioning everyone that's selling weed and coke. He even tried to question me, but I ain't tell him shit. I put my hand on my shit."

"AR, you're crazy. You know that's Mello's dad."

As AR spoke, it hit him. He remembered running into Mack's room and seeing the duffle bag full of weed and the two squares wrapped up in black tape. Lo wondered if his brother was involved in the robbery. Why would he cross Zeus? He helped him rob Rico. Lo's thoughts were cloudy, so he changed the subject, interrupting AR.

"Have you seen Jazzy or Jenny?"

"That's another thing. Jazzy has been looking for you. Last I heard she was on her way to Massachusetts for the summer to see her dad."

"Damn, I hope not. I bought her something. I wanted to give it to her."

Lo pulled the gift that he bought her out of his pocket, revealing the heart ring with Jazzy's initials on it and the Mickey Mouse chain.

"Damn, son, you went hard on her. Your lil ass is really in love," AR joked.

"Nah, I'm not in love. I just wanted her to have something to think about me."

Lo and AR headed toward the park. Kim and Sandy were sitting on their stoop when they walked up.

"Have you seen Jazzy?" Lo asked.

"She just stopped by to say her goodbyes before she left. She was looking for you," Kim said.

"I don't know why," Sandy chimed in with an agitated voice.

Lo gave her a dirty look then said, "Did she leave yet?"

"Let me call her," Kim said as she ran into the house to get her iPhone.

Lo started to pray in his mind as Kim disappeared. Sandy gave Lo a stank look. Lo ignored her. It seemed like Kim was taking forever as he waited impatiently, looking from side to side. From a distance Lo spotted a figure walking toward the park. Even from a distance she was beautiful. She wore a white T-shirt, a pair of blue jean booty shorts that showed off every inch of her caramel skin legs, and white Air Forces. Kim must not have told her that he was there, because when she saw him, she darted through the park. As she got closer, arms opened, Lo extended his arms as Jazzy leaped into them. He swung her around, lifting her off her feet, giving her a warm "I miss you" kiss.

"Why are you leaving me, and when are you coming back?"

"I'm leaving tonight to my father's house. Then I'm going to my grandmother's in Puerto Rico. I'll be gone the whole summer. I'm sorry. I'm gonna miss you so much."

Lo squeezed her tightly. "I'm gonna miss you, too, but before you leave, I bought you something. When you look at it, I want you to think of me."

He went into his pocket and pulled out the two boxes. A huge smile came across her face. Before she spoke a word, she placed a wet kiss on his lips.

"I love you, Lo."

Lo was caught off guard. He didn't know what to say. He had a lot of feelings for her, but love? He never thought that he would be telling her that, but he just went with the flow.

"I love you too, Jazzy." He kissed her again. It was a deep sensual one too.

"Awwww," Kim yelled, watching the two of them have an intimate moment.

As the couple turned toward Kim, Lo noticed Sandy had her arms crossed grilling Jazzy. Jazzy smirked her face at her. She knew Sandy was obsessed with Lo, but he was all hers. So she rubbed a smile in Sandy's face.

"It's okay, bitch. You'll be gone a whole fucking summer and watch what I got planned," Sandy mumbled to herself, with revenge on her mind.

Lo and Jazzy walked off hand in hand leaving AR at Kim's. Lo spent the rest of the day with Jazzy. He forgot about his re-up, because he just wanted to cherish the moment with her.

NINETEEN

RICKY PUT THE GLASS TUBE TO HIS LIPS, STRUCK the lighter and inhaled the crack into his lungs. He then passed the tube and lighter to Pretty Boy. Not in a million years would Mack have thought his right-hand man would turn into a crackhead.

"This is that fire that Mack got," Ricky said as he exhaled the crack smoke.

As Pretty Boy exhaled the crack smoke, his ears popped. The high hit him instantly.

"Damn, this shit is good. I'ma need some of this for the block. What's the prices on this shit?"

Ricky's jaw was locked as he tried to respond. "Woo, woo, one twenty-five a ba, ba, ball, and eight an ounce."

"Damn, that's cheap. I'ma need an ounce," Pretty Boy said.

Ricky continued to fill the glass tube. Rock after rock. He didn't realize how much the two had smoked. It was three in the morning and the high was calm. Ricky questioned Pretty Boy about Zeus.

"What's up with Zeus? I haven't seen him since I got shot. He's been ducking me."

"Nah, Ricky. It's not like that. Zeus been fucked up. A few weeks ago, the stash spot got hit. So he's been running around trying to make money."

"What? Who got him? Why nobody told me? What they get?"

"They got him for all that work from the Easton nigga. Shit put a dent in his pockets."

In life, karma's a muthafucka, and Ricky didn't even think of it. They continued to speak on the robbery and how shit didn't fall into place. Then there was a knock on the door. When Ricky answered it, it was some lady that lived down the street from them. She was wearing a skimpy skirt and tank top. She smelled the crack and wanted some. Since she didn't have any money, they had other things in mind. When she came in and sat down, Ricky and Pretty Boy could see that she wasn't wearing panties. They passed her the tube and lighter.

"Hit this shit, so we can hit that pussy."

She took a couple of pulls, and her eyes closed as she leaned back on the bed. She was feeling the effects already. Pretty Boy was the first to get closer to her. He lifted her already short skirt up to her waist, exposing her clean-shaved pussy. Both of them instantly bricked up.

"Come on, because I have to get back home before my husband gets off of work," she said, opening her legs wider for them to get a better view of her goodies.

Ricky walked over to where her face was, while Pretty Boy started eating her pussy. She took Ricky's dick into her mouth, and the warmness almost had him cumming immediately. Pretty Boy could smell a pissy scent coming from her vagina, but he didn't care about it. All he wanted to do was fuck the beautiful lady. After a couple of minutes of licking the pussy, he pulled down his pants and entered her raw. He didn't even think about wearing a condom.

"Damn, you gotta get some of this. Her shit is fire, Ricky," Pretty Boy said as he continued pumping away. He was on the verge of busting a nut. "How's her head game?"

Ricky's eyes closed as he enjoyed the warmness of her tongue working its magic around the tip of his dick. "This shit is off the chain, bro."

Pretty Boy lifted her legs up to his shoulders so he could really kill it. He was trying his best to make his dick touch her stomach.

"Please, I can't stand it, baby. I'm begging you, please hurry up and cum," she panted as she stopped sucking Ricky's dick to talk to Pretty Boy.

Her screams were washed away by her moaning and

groaning, just as he knew they would be each time he filled her up with all ten inches. Each stroke was slow and sensual. It didn't take either one of them long to reach the climax they had been anticipating. He came inside her.

Once he was done, they switched positions. Ricky did the same thing and entered her without a condom. If it wasn't for the crack, they probably would have been thinking.

"Oh my God, you're so big," she moaned, feeling her walls being stretched as he pumped in and out of her. He didn't last more than two minutes before he also shot his load inside her.

Once they were done with the woman, she got up off the bed and left. Pretty Boy did the same, but not before they had another hit of the crack. Ricky was so high that he fell asleep right in the bed that all of their semen was on. He didn't care.

With a few hours of sleep, Ricky showered up, got

dressed and headed to the Gardens. It was collection day. Every Sunday, Mack would collect the week's earnings. Ricky knew that he would be in the doghouse after smoking almost an ounce of crack with Pretty Boy and the lady from down the street.

Five o'clock came quick. Ricky collected from each of his runners: $3,000 apiece off four $1,000 packs. If they took no shorts, the runners would have easily pocketed a stack, so everybody ate. Even after smoking the 21 grams, Ricky's count was still correct. He still had work from the quarter brick that Mack gave him, and 160 grams had been chopped up for the runners.

That left 90 for Ricky. He had smoked 21, which left him with almost 70 grams to play with. He was to report $12,500 back to Juice for Mack. He got twelve stacks. He was in debt for five hundred. It didn't seem like much to a hustler, but it's all about stacking in the game. All Ricky wanted to do was get high and smoke all his profit. He did all his collections, then left to the south side.

~ ~ ~

"You collected everything from everyone?" Mack asked Juice as he smoked.

"I seen Vic and Husky. They peeled me the twelve five for the work, and eight for the bud. Off the eight, I gave them back twenty-five hundred and told them to split it down the middle."

"What about Ricky?"

"I still haven't collected anything from him yet. He was out there collecting, then he disappeared. I got ten from my spot, and five from the weed. Have you heard from him?"

"Nah, I haven't seen him since the party. I've been hanging with Erica. She's a handful. But I'll get up with him. In the meantime, how're things with Fat Freddy?"

"He's been feeling the pressure. I guess he thinks that we will eventually run out and then he'll be back on top again. He still has his loyal customers," Juice said.

"Good. As long as everyone is eating. Is everybody out?"

"Rob and I are. Vic and Husky should be almost out. I'll check on that."

"Aiight. I'm a head out, grab some more work, then make a move. I'll be back in a couple hours. I'll stop by Ricky's too." Mack gave Juice a pound and hopped in his car. "I hope Ricky didn't fuck up the money," he said out loud.

He knew that Ricky wouldn't betray him, but he wasn't dealing with Ricky anymore. He was now dealing with Ricky on crack, and the crack would make a fiend turn on his own mother if she got in the way of him getting high. Mack's mind was going in circles as he headed across town. His mind was on the $12,000 Ricky had. He placed his system on five, so he could barely hear his subwoofers thump.

Riding with $33,000, tinted windows, through the

middle of Center City at seven at night was an easy target for the cops. He hit every alley until he reached Ricky's house. As Mack pulled up, he noticed a black Expedition with four dudes inside, sitting four houses away from Ricky's house. He slowly drove past the SUV without stopping. He took a glance inside the SUV's window, trying to see a face. The driver had a fitted cap that lay low over his eyes, which made it hard for him to recognize the person. He noticed something else that caught his eye: it was the bright orange *H* that sat on the fitted cap.

Houston Astros hats are known to be worn by members of the Hole. Mack was confused. Was Zeus plotting on Ricky, or were they waiting on him? He circled the block and parked six cars behind the black SUV. After ten minutes of surveillance, the black SUV pulled out of the parking space, without anyone getting in.

Forgetting about the $33,000 in his possession, he pulled out and followed the SUV. It headed toward Big Poppa's spot. Mack was so caught up with following the

SUV, that he didn't notice the Chevy Astro that had pulled up beside him. It was too late. All Mack heard was the shots in the air.

POP! POP! POP! POP! POP! POP! POP! POP! POP! POP!

Mack's car was riddled with bullets. He stepped on the gas pedal. More shots rang out, hitting his vehicle three more times. He swerved his car side to side like a slithering snake as he dodged the bullets and played chicken with the traffic.

Mack felt hot liquid coming down his face. The first thing he thought was that he was shot, but didn't know where. His face was leaking, but it wasn't enough for him to stop. He was still conscious, and his adrenaline was pumping. He was mad because he was caught once again off guard.

Blood covered his eyes as he wiped them in order to see. He pulled into an empty parking spot outside his house. Face bloody, he popped the trunk and grabbed the money. He looked at his riddled car. It was a wonder that he wasn't dead right now. Mack jogged to his house, touching his body and making sure he didn't have any bullet holes. He opened the door and slammed it shut behind him.

"Mack, what happened to you?" Lo yelled as he watched Mack take a couple more steps before falling to the floor in a puddle of his own blood.

DEATH BY ASSOCIATION

PART 2

COMING SOON

To order books, please fill out the order form below:
To order films please go to www.good2gofilms.com

Name:_____

Address:_____

City:_____State:_____Zip Code: _____

Phone:_____

Email:_____

Method of Payment: Check   VISA MASTERCARD

Credit Card#:_ _____

Name as it appears on card: _____

Signature: _____

Item Name	Price	Qty	Amount
48 Hours to Die – Silk White	$14.99		
A Hustler's Dream - Ernest Morris	$14.99		
A Hustler's Dream 2 - Ernest Morris	$14.99		
A Thug's Devotion – J. L. Rose and J. M. McMillon	$14.99		
All Eyes on Tommy Gunz – Warren Holloway	$14.99		
Black Reign – Ernest Morris	$14.99		
Bloody Mayhem Down South – Trayvon Jackson	$14.99		
Bloody Mayhem Down South 2 – Trayvon Jackson	$14.99		
Business Is Business – Silk White	$14.99		
Business Is Business 2 – Silk White	$14.99		
Business Is Business 3 – Silk White	$14.99		
Cash In Cash Out – Assa Raymond Baker	$14.99		
Cash In Cash Out 2 - Assa Raymond Baker	$14.99		
Childhood Sweethearts – Jacob Spears	$14.99		
Childhood Sweethearts 2 – Jacob Spears	$14.99		
Childhood Sweethearts 3 - Jacob Spears	$14.99		
Childhood Sweethearts 4 - Jacob Spears	$14.99		
Connected To The Plug – Dwan Marquis Williams	$14.99		
Connected To The Plug 2 – Dwan Marquis Williams	$14.99		
Connected To The Plug 3 – Dwan Williams	$14.99		
Cost of Betrayal – W.C. Holloway	$14.99		
Cost of Betrayal 2 – W.C. Holloway	$14.99		
Deadly Reunion – Ernest Morris	$14.99		
Death by Association	$14.99		
Dream's Life – Assa Raymond Baker	$14.99		
Flipping Numbers – Ernest Morris	$14.99		

Flipping Numbers 2 – Ernest Morris	$14.99		
He Loves Me, He Loves You Not - Mychea	$14.99		
He Loves Me, He Loves You Not 2 - Mychea	$14.99		
He Loves Me, He Loves You Not 3 - Mychea	$14.99		
He Loves Me, He Loves You Not 4 – Mychea	$14.99		
He Loves Me, He Loves You Not 5 – Mychea	$14.99		
Killing Signs – Ernest Morris	$14.99		
Killing Signs 2 – Ernest Morris	$14.99		
Kings of the Block – Dwan Willams	$14.99		
Kings of the Block 2 – Dwan Willams	$14.99		
Lord of My Land – Jay Morrison	$14.99		
Lost and Turned Out – Ernest Morris	$14.99		
Love & Dedication – W.C. Holloway	$14.99		
Love Hates Violence – De'Wayne Maris	$14.99		
Love Hates Violence 2 – De'Wayne Maris	$14.99		
Love Hates Violence 3 – De'Wayne Maris	$14.99		
Love Hates Violence 4 – De'Wayne Maris	$14.99		
Married To Da Streets – Silk White	$14.99		
M.E.R.C. - Make Every Rep Count Health and Fitness	$14.99		
Mercenary In Love – J.L. Rose & J.L. Turner	$14.99		
Money Make Me Cum – Ernest Morris	$14.99		
My Besties – Asia Hill	$14.99		
My Besties 2 – Asia Hill	$14.99		
My Besties 3 – Asia Hill	$14.99		
My Besties 4 – Asia Hill	$14.99		
My Boyfriend's Wife - Mychea	$14.99		
My Boyfriend's Wife 2 – Mychea	$14.99		
My Brothers Envy – J. L. Rose	$14.99		
My Brothers Envy 2 – J. L. Rose	$14.99		
Naughty Housewives – Ernest Morris	$14.99		
Naughty Housewives 2 – Ernest Morris	$14.99		
Naughty Housewives 3 – Ernest Morris	$14.99		
Naughty Housewives 4 – Ernest Morris	$14.99		
Never Be The Same – Silk White	$14.99		
Scarred Knuckles – Assa Raymond Baker	$14.99		

Scarred Knuckles 2 – Assa Raymond Baker	$14.99		
Shades of Revenge – Assa Raymond Baker	$14.99		
Slumped – Jason Brent	$14.99		
Someone's Gonna Get It – Mychea	$14.99		
Stranded – Silk White	$14.99		
Supreme & Justice – Ernest Morris	$14.99		
Supreme & Justice 2 – Ernest Morris	$14.99		
Supreme & Justice 3 – Ernest Morris	$14.99		
Tears of a Hustler - Silk White	$14.99		
Tears of a Hustler 2 - Silk White	$14.99		
Tears of a Hustler 3 - Silk White	$14.99		
Tears of a Hustler 4- Silk White	$14.99		
Tears of a Hustler 5 – Silk White	$14.99		
Tears of a Hustler 6 – Silk White	$14.99		
The Last Love Letter – Warren Holloway	$14.99		
The Last Love Letter 2 – Warren Holloway	$14.99		
The Panty Ripper - Reality Way	$14.99		
The Panty Ripper 3 – Reality Way	$14.99		
The Solution – Jay Morrison	$14.99		
The Teflon Queen – Silk White	$14.99		
The Teflon Queen 2 – Silk White	$14.99		
The Teflon Queen 3 – Silk White	$14.99		
The Teflon Queen 4 – Silk White	$14.99		
The Teflon Queen 5 – Silk White	$14.99		
The Teflon Queen 6 - Silk White	$14.99		
The Vacation – Silk White	$14.99		
Tied To A Boss - J.L. Rose	$14.99		
Tied To A Boss 2 - J.L. Rose	$14.99		
Tied To A Boss 3 - J.L. Rose	$14.99		
Tied To A Boss 4 - J.L. Rose	$14.99		
Tied To A Boss 5 - J.L. Rose	$14.99		
Time Is Money - Silk White	$14.99		
Tomorrow's Not Promised – Robert Torres	$14.99		
Tomorrow's Not Promised 2 – Robert Torres	$14.99		
Two Mask One Heart – Jacob Spears and Trayvon Jackson	$14.99		
Two Mask One Heart 2 – Jacob Spears and Trayvon Jackson	$14.99		

Two Mask One Heart 3 – Jacob Spears and Trayvon Jackson	$14.99		
Wrong Place Wrong Time – Silk White	$14.99		
Young Goonz – Reality Way	$14.99		
Subtotal:			
Tax:			
Shipping (Free) U.S. Media Mail:			
Total:			

Make Checks Payable To: Good2Go Publishing, 7311 W Glass Lane, Laveen, AZ 85339

9 781947 340572